9 STORIE

translated from the Urdu by
**Vibha S. Chauhan
and Khalid Alvi**

Published by
Rupa Publications India Pvt. Ltd 2014
7/16, Ansari Road, Daryaganj
New Delhi 110002

Sales centres:
Allahabad Bengaluru Chennai
Hyderabad Jaipur Kathmandu
Kolkata Mumbai

Translation copyright © Khalid Alvi and Vibha S. Chauhan

The copyright of the original stories remain with the respective authors or their estates.

This is a work of fiction. Names, characters, places and incidents are either the product of the author's imagination or are used fictitiously, and any resemblance to any actual persons, living or dead, events or locales is entirely coincidental.

All rights reserved.
No part of this publication may be reproduced, transmitted, or stored in a retrieval system, in any form or by any means, electronic, mechanical, photocopying, recording or otherwise, without the prior permission of the publisher.

ISBN: 978-81-291-3108-9

10 9 8 7 6 5 4 3 2 1

The moral right of the authors has been asserted.

Printed at Replika Press Pvt. Ltd., India

This book is sold subject to the condition that it shall not, by way of trade or otherwise, be lent, resold, hired out, or otherwise circulated, without the publisher's prior consent, in any form of binding or cover other than that in which it is published.

Vibha S. Chauhan teaches English at the Zakir Husain Delhi College, University of Delhi. Her research interests include translation and indigenous cultures and societies. She has written a novel in Hindi, *Ganga Jamuna Beech* and translated Joginder Paul's Urdu novel *Paar Pare* into English, published as *Beyond Black Waters*. She has penned *Maa Siddeshwari*, a biography of the legendary singer Siddeshwari Devi, as well as a book on cultural diversity. Proficient in Bhojpuri, she is at present translating a Bhojpuri epic into English.

Khalid Alvi teaches Urdu at Zakir Husain Delhi College. Though a specialist in the ghazal form, Khalid has lectured widely on various other aspects of Urdu literature and historiography both within and outside India. Khalid collected and compiled the first edition of *Angarey* in Urdu, before which it was not available at all. His collection of articles, *Baazyaft*, is widely read. His book *Qayam Chandpuri* talks about the eighteenth-century poet Qayam, whom Ghalib held in high esteem.

Contents

Foreword	*vii*
Introduction	*xv*
A Summer Night *Sajjad Zahir*	1
Dulari *Sajjad Zahir*	10
Heaven Assured! *Sajjad Zahir*	17
Insomnia *Sajjad Zahir*	25
The Same Uproar, Once Again *Sajjad Zahir*	38
A Trip to Delhi *Rashid Jahan*	49

Masculinity	53
Mahmuduzzafar	
The Clouds Don't Come	62
Ahmed Ali	
A Night of Winter Rain	73
Ahmed Ali	
Behind the Veil: A One-Act Play	83
Rashid Jahan	
Acknowledgements	103

Foreword

The publication of the English translation of *Angarey* is truly a very special occasion for me. It has, in one stroke, transported me back to the world of my parents, their constant struggle against injustice and inequality, and their undying hope of ushering in a world order where personal fulfillment is not at odds with social upliftment. The search for a just society continues and is as vital today as it was in 1932, the year *Angarey* was first published.

In 1932, Abba, my father Sajjad Zahir, was a young man and had just returned to India after studying in England. During his stay there, he had come into contact with many progressive writers and thinkers from different parts of Europe. His combat zone, however, was his own country where he dreamt of creating a world free from social, economic and religious exploitation. It was his friendship with like-minded people like Ahmed Ali, Rashid Jahan and

Angarey

Mahmuduzzafar, all of whom believed in the power of the written word to change the world, that made the publication of *Angarey* possible. Though the collection was published many years before any of my three sisters or I was born, it remained alive for us both as a symbol of courage to seek a new world free of all discrimination as well as the unending challenge that confronts one in the process.

Abba could have written in English with great ease but his decision to write in Urdu was a conscious and well-considered one. Urdu, according to him, represented the 'Ganga-Jamuni tehzeeb', or the diverse tongues and cultures of the people of India. He had published a few short stories in some Urdu journals before the publication of *Angarey* and remained involved with the world of writing and publishing all his life. Despite this, *Angarey* remained his most cherished, emotional and ambitious project. It brought him in contact with friends and intellectuals who shared his worldview and gave him a foretaste of the forces which he would meet, confront and challenge all through his life. These included the stranglehold that restricted not just society but the world of literature, writing, theatre and performance, too. The young group of writers of *Angarey* challenged not just social orthodoxy but also traditional literary narratives and techniques. In an attempt to represent the individual mind and its struggle, they ushered in the narrative technique known as the stream of consciousness which was then new to the contemporary literary scene and continues to be significant in literature even today.

Foreword

It is needless to say that *Angarey* and the issues it deals with have had a deep impact on my writings as well as the theatre that I have been involved with. As little girls, my sisters and I had hardly realized the significance of the poets, writers, ideologues and the ideas which reverberated through our home. The notions, concepts and struggles that were part of the lives of people we saw, met and played with, existed around us as naturally and as unobtrusively as the air we breathe. It was not something that was constructed consciously for our inculcation. Yet, probably the most effective and effortless process of education is that in which we learn, absorb and assimilate values without being aware of them.

Our upbringing was as uninhibited and unregimented as it could have been. No subject was a taboo and no boundaries regarding our personal and professional lives were set by our parents. Each one of us was left free to chart out our own lives and so we did.

It is only later in life that we became aware of the significance of our upbringing in the midst of a group of creative people who saw art as a means of social reform. When I look at my own career in theatre, I realize how I have steered towards the concept of interaction between aesthetics and social theatre through the kind of plays I have acted in, written, produced and directed. I have written seven plays without being fully conscious of the inheritance of my childhood. Yet, I find that they focus on prevalent social issues. If I now look at the plays that I have written with an outsider's gaze, I am amazed to find how they

Angarey

become connected to some of the themes that raise their heads in *Angarey*. My plays such as *Saku-Bai* and *Daya Shankar ki Dairy* discuss significant social issues. *Suman aur Sana* focuses on communal harmony with half the play set in Kashmir and the other half in Ahmedabad. *Operation Cloudburst* deals with the military operation in Northeast India. *Yaar Bana Buddy*, as the title suggests, discusses the impact of consumerism and Westernization on our culture and relationships. The condition and status of women is the focus of the play *Ji, Jaisi Aapki Marzi*. A recapitulation of the history of art through cinema and the impact of technology on cinema becomes the theme of my play *Salaam* which deals with the era of black-and-white films and attempts to establish how these films managed to deliver their messages despite being technically not as sophisticated as the films of today

Thus, my plays and many of their themes are actually an extension of the issues highlighted in *Angarey*. In that sense, these stories are as relevant today as they were at the time when the collection was published. The response to the collection would not have been so aggressive had it not touched some live nerve among people. I feel that it is therefore fortunate that the collection is being translated into English for I hope that this will take it to a much wider set of readers—especially the youth—who I trust will be inspired to make our society better, more just and more equitable as did that young group of writers who risked their lives when they wrote and published *Angarey*.

Ammi, my mother Razia Sajjad Zahir, was a prominent

Foreword

writer and translator in her own right and she and my father together lived the life that they advocated through their writings. It was after her marriage to my father that my mother studied and completed her master's degree from Allahabad. The two supported each other in a relationship that was founded on shared dreams and mutual respect. My parents were physically separated for almost half of the thirty-five years of their married lives due to my father's travelling for political work or due to the time he spent in jail. Ammi took over all the responsibilities of home and family during these times and still continued to write. The merit of her work can be gauged from the awards she received, such as the Nehru Award in 1966 and the Uttar Pradesh State Sahitya Akademi Award in 1972. She belonged to the small group of women writers of the time that included Ismat Chughtai, Rashid Jahan and Siddiqa Begum Sevharvi who openly defied and contested existing social constraints.

However, there were times when her nerves were tested beyond limits. One such phase was when Abba was arrested in connection with the Rawalpindi Conspiracy Case in Pakistan. He was, in fact, awarded a death sentence and extradited back to India only on the request of Jawaharlal Nehru. He hardly talked about the details regarding his imprisonment and it was from another compatriot that we got to know how when in Pakistan, he had refused to change his locale to protect a friend who had known about his whereabouts.

Angarey and all that it signifies has never been far from our lives. In fact, the collection often came up for discussion

Angarey

by friends of my parents, sometimes in all seriousness and sometimes even in good humour. Kaifi Azmi, I remember, used to laugh and narrate how he and his classmates at school believed that his maulana used to read *Angarey* in secret. Qamar Rais often discussed the impact that *Angarey* had on writings of other writers of the Progressive Writers' Association citing stories like Premchand's 'Miss Padma' and 'Kafan' as examples. Some others also believed that the title of Manto's first collection of short stories *Aatish Paare* was also inspired by *Angarey*.

However, whenever Abba looked back at the time of *Angarey*, he did not think of its writing and the problems that followed as any kind of hardship or sacrifice. Rather, for him as well as for the other writers of the collection, it provided them with the opportunity of expressing truths simply felt and clearly articulated. This was also exactly the way I feel they lived their lives—simply, honestly and fearlessly.

Angarey being reborn in its English avatar, I feel, brings back the theme of social reform going hand in hand with creativity. Given its idiom and complexity, it could not have been an easy book to translate. I congratulate both Vibha S. Chauhan and Khalid Alvi who, through their translation, will take the original collection to a much wider readership. I believe that the translation will also be successful in bringing back *Angarey* into the academic discourse as being the first manifestation of the aesthetic expression that grew into the much better known Progressive Writers' Association. By drawing our attention back to *Angarey* and connecting it to

Foreword

the history of progressive writing, both Vibha S. Chauhan and Khalid Alvi have filled a serious gap and made the story of the connection between writing, creativity and social ethos more inclusive and comprehensive.

Nadira Z. Babbar
September 2013

Introduction

Angarey: The Controversy

'*Angarey* was not just a mere collection of short stories but a sophisticated protest against established traditions and conventions. It was a declaration of a path-breaking testament.'[1]
 —QAMAR RAIS

Angarey was first published in December 1932 by the Nizami Press, Lucknow. In March 1933, the government of the United Provinces banned *Angarey* four months later. However, even after *Angarey* was proscribed, the four young contributors to the volume—Sajjad Zahir, Ahmed Ali, Rashid Jahan and Mahmuduzzafar—refused to apologize

---

[1]'Urdu mein Angarey ki Ravayat' in *Tanquidi Tanazur*, p. 65.

Angarey

for it. On 5 April 1933, Mahmuduzzafar wrote an article, 'In Defence of *Angarey*' for *The Leader*, a newspaper published from Allahabad. The piece was also reproduced in some other papers, including the *Hindustan Times*. Subtitled 'Shall We Submit to Gagging?' it lashes out against the muzzling of free speech. The article is neither an apology nor an expression of fear. On the contrary, it reiterates the 'inner indignation' against 'the sorry scheme of things' that had found expression in *Angarey*. It ends with a call for 'the formation immediately of a league of progressive authors which should bring forth similar collections from time to time, both in English and the various vernaculars of our country'. Thus, *Angarey* is much more than an expression of youthful defiance. It marks a defining moment, not just in Urdu literature, but in literatures of the many other languages of India. *Angarey* also laid the foundation of the Progressive Writers' Association, which is by far the most significant literary movement to have sprung up in twentieth-century India. Most of all, the volume forged a kind of literary consciousness which perceives aesthetic expression as being integrally fused with political and social codes. This consciousness has a continuing impact on literature even today.

It is evident that none of the four writers of the collection were at any point oblivious of the social and political chastisement that would follow its publication. Nonetheless, what is also true is that they had underestimated the severity and extent of hostility it actually generated. Ahmed Ali affirms this in several interviews when he says, 'We knew

Introduction

the book would create a stir but never dreamt that it would bring the house down.'[2]

The passionate intensity of the controversy that erupted after the publication of *Angarey* becomes evident when one traces the war of words which took place in the United Provinces. The *Hindustan Times* ran an article on 23 February 1933 titled 'Urdu Pamphlet Denounced: Shias Gravely Upset':

> The following resolution has been passed by the Central Standing Committee of the All-India Shia Conference at a meeting held on Sunday last:-
> The Central Standing Committee of the All-India Shia Conference at this meeting strongly condemns the heart-rending and filthy pamphlet called 'Angare' compiled by Sajjad Zahir, Ahmad Ali, Rashid Jehan and Mahmadul Zafar which has wounded the feelings of the entire Muslim community by ridiculing God and his Prophets and which is extremely objectionable from the standpoints of both religion and morality. The Committee further strongly urges upon the attention of the U.P. Government that the book be at once proscribed.

Many Urdu newspapers and journals, too, criticized *Angarey* as being obscene and blasphemous and stridently demanded its proscription. Hafiz Maulvi Hidayat Husain, a member

---

[2] Quoted in Carlo Coppola, 'The Angare Group: The Enfant Terribles of Urdu Literature', *Annals of Urdu Studies*, Volume I, 1981, p.61.

Angarey

of the U.P. Council, raised his voice against the book in the council on 27 February 1933 and demanded that the book be taken off the shelves. In response to his demand, Sir Ahmed Saeed Khan, home member, assured him that the government would take immediate action against the book.[3] The city magistrate of Lucknow summoned Mirza Mohammad Jawwad, the owner of the Nizami Press which printed *Angarey*, and had him declare in court, under oath, that he had inadvertently hurt the religious sentiments of people and had him offer an apology for doing so. The notification which demanded the removal of copies of *Angarey* from the stands was published on 15 March 1933 in the State Gazette.

**POLICE DEPARTMENT
MISCELLANEOUS**

15th March, 1933

No.98/VIII—1031—In exercise of the power conferred by Section 99A of the Code of Criminal Procedure, 1898 (Act V of 1898), the Governor in Council hereby declares to be forfeited to His Majesty every copy of a book in Urdu entitled 'Angare' written by Sayed Sajjad Zahir, Ahmad Ali, Rashid Jahan and Mahmudal Zafar, published by Sajjad Zahir, Butlerganj, Lucknow, and printed by Mirza Mohammad Jawwad at the Nizami

---

[3]*Sarfaraz*, Lucknow, 28 February 1933.

Introduction

Press, Victoria Street, Lucknow on the ground that the said book contains matter the publication of which is punishable under section 295A of the Indian Penal Code.

As soon as he was told of the decision of the government, Mohammad Jawwad promptly sent all copies of the collection to the office of the city magistrate. These copies were set on fire under Act 295-A of the Indian Penal Code (1860).[4]

Copies of *Angarey* were available to the reading public as well as to scholars for a very brief period of time, yet this was enough to divide them into sharply conflicting groups. A respected contemporary scholar and critic, Akhtar Hussain Raipuri, wrote a fifteen-page long review under his pen name, Naqqad, praising *Angarey*. This review was published in the journal, *Urdu*, which was edited by the eminent scholar Maulvi Abdul Haq.[5] Maulvi Abdul Haq was a serious researcher who has published and edited several ancient scripts and has also compiled several dictionaries. Munshi Dayanarain Nigam was the other prominent supporter of *Angarey*. He edited the monthly Urdu magazine *Zamana* which

---

[4]Whoever, with deliberate and malicious intention of outraging the religious feelings of any class of His Majesty's subjects, by words, either spoken or written, or by visual representations, insults, or attempts to insult the religion or the religious beliefs of that class, shall be punished with imprisonment of either description for a term which may extend to two years, or with fine, or with both.
[5]*Urdu*, Aurangabad, April 1933, p. 413.

published several prominent writers of the time such as Premchand and Dr Iqbal.[6]

Another prominent defender of the book was Professor Mohammad Mujib who taught at Jamia Millia Islamia when Zakir Husain, the former President of India, was its vice-chancellor. Rahman wrote a three-page review under the pen name Meem in the magazine *Jamia Monthly*. Two short stories by Sajjad Zahir had also been published in *Jamia Monthly* before they found a place in *Angarey*. Mujib praises the stories written by Sajjad Zahir and, quoting long extracts from 'Garmiyon ki ek raat' and 'Jannat ki Basharat', describes them as being the best stories in the volume.[7] What is noteworthy about the article, however, is that it recognizes literature as a means of criticizing social ills and 'ushering in reforms'; an idea that reverberates in the aesthetic credo of the writers themselves. This is clearly evident when he writes:

> *Angarey* is 'angare', glowing coals—and not merely stories—in the true sense! These do not present life as such but a special kind of existence. Their purpose is to impact our senses in a very unique way—to burn and demolish much that exists in our society. The existing thoughts, faith, social values have been ridiculed in some places and their weaknesses and demerits have been identified in others. Stark images of poverty,

---

[6]*Zamana*, Kanpur, May 1933. p.33.

[7]'Tanquid-o-tabsara', *Jamia Monthly*, Delhi, February 1933.

Introduction

helplessness, vulnerability and illiteracy present in Muslim society co-exist with this. There is also a clear protest against the tyranny of the empowered classes. Our social values and predilections must not obsess us to the extent that we begin to perceive difference of opinion as disrespect of these values. An absence of freedom to criticize results in the impossibility of ushering in reforms. The arrogance that sees criticism as humiliation, differences as enmity, and the informal expression of thought as impertinence is the strongest enemy of sincerity and faith. However, it is the basic duty of every creative person to carefully investigate whether or not the form of criticism and protest selected fulfills that special purpose. Verbal abuse is also a way of expressing one's thoughts and emotions and we cannot take away the right to use this kind of abuse from someone who has been gifted of speech by Allah. All the same, everybody realizes the extent to which these are able to convey our feelings and thoughts. There are certainly different ways of ridiculing.

The opponents of *Angarey* were no less eloquent.[8] Many booksellers were reported to have returned the copies of the book without even displaying them in their stores for fear of 'irreparable damage' to their business. Others claimed that many booksellers fainted at the mere sight of the book.

---

[8] Carlo Coppola, p. 62.

Angarey

Some others were much harsher and declared that writers of a book as offensive as *Angarey* must not be spared at all and be punished with 'stoning and if need be, hanging'.[9]

Newspapers like the English daily *Star*, published from Allahabad, condemned *Angarey* in no uncertain terms. Many Urdu newspapers and magazines published similar critical articles and responses. *Sach* (published from Lucknow); the daily *Khilafat* (published from Lucknow), the bi-weekly *Sarfaraz* (published from Lucknow), *Payam* (published from Aligarh), *Hum-dum* (published from Lucknow), *Naved* (published from Lucknow), *Azad* (published from Lahore), *Rahbar-e-Daccan* (published from Hyderabad), *Shiraza* (published from Barabanki), *Mukbir-e-alam* (published from Muradabad), *Madina* (published from Bijnore), and the daily *Haqeeqat* (published from Lucknow) all published several articles which severely criticized the book. Some others tried to strike a balance. For instance, *Haqeeqat* published a note against *Angarey* but simultaneously carried a letter in its support, which tried to argue that *Angarey* must be looked at from the technical point of view and be kept at a distance from religion.

But the two newspapers which managed to turn the criticism against *Angarey* into a movement against the book were *Sach* and *Sarfaraz*. In an attempt to vilify *Angarey*, Maulana Majid Dariyabadi, the editor of *Sach*, claimed to have met

---

[9]Ahmed Ali, 'The Progressive Writers' Movement in its Historical Perspective', *Journal of South Asian Literature*, Volume I, 1981, p.92.

Introduction

Premchand on a train journey and to have shown him a copy of *Angarey*. He reports that Premchand called the book dirty, obscene and vulgar.

Perfunctory research into the whereabouts of Premchand at this time reveals that this incident could have taken place only between 21 and 28 April 1933. *Sach* was a weekly and yet this meeting also did not find mention in the preceding issue even though it had carried an article on *Angarey*. A further examination of Premchand's own accounts, as well as those of his friends and contemporaries, reveals that the incident probably never occurred since Premchand had not travelled out of Banaras during that period. All records indicate that on 21 April 1933, Premchand had written a letter from Banaras to Vishnu Prabhakar regarding Prabhakar's article which was to be published in *Jagaran*, the journal Premchand edited. On 24 April, he published an advertisement about the launch of *Jagaran* from Lucknow. He was in Banaras on 26 April when he received the news of the birth of his grandson. On 1 May, he also received, via a telegram, news that Kamala Devi, his daughter, was running a fever on 29 and 30 April. These facts prove conclusively that during this period, Premchand went on only one journey from Banaras to Allahabad in the month of February.

Premchand's statements and personal responses to various issues, including articles and books, were quite frank. He had criticized Acharya Chatursen Shastri's *Islam ka Vishvriksha* in unambiguous terms as having being written

Angarey

for a little money and a little fame.[10]

The Creation and the Creators of Angarey

The comment in *Haqueeqat* regarding the distinctiveness of 'the technical point of view' of the stories in *Angarey* seeks to draw our attention to the text itself which broke new ground as far as the strategies of narration and form are concerned. The writers, while keenly sensitive to the socio-political location of the characters in their narratives, also invite readers to step into their minds and trace the movement of their thoughts and feelings. In doing so, the writers were self-consciously challenging the traditional literary conventions of representation and experimenting with techniques which allowed them to fuse together the formlessness of thought processes with the solidity of social realism. The stories delve deep into the dark recesses of the human mind to reveal the individual psyche through the written word. Coupled with non-sequential jigs of memory and the absence of structured punctuation, the collection brings to mind the writings of some of the major Western modern novelists such as James Joyce, Virginia Woolf and William Faulkner. Even a brief examination of the lives of the four writers reveals their active interaction with the political and literary milieu of the West as well as the lived realities of India at that time.

---

[10] Amrit Rai, *Premchand: Vividh Prasang* (Allahabad: Hansa Prakashan, 1962), p. 416.

Introduction

Sajjad Zahir (1905-1973) was the moving spirit behind *Angarey* and the collection includes five stories written by him. He collected and edited the other four stories and the play as well. The son of a prominent judge of the High Court of Judicature, Allahabad, Sajjad Zahir has an interesting career chart which represents the complex interconnections between contemporary Western and Indian thought and aesthetics. While still in India, his attraction towards Marxism had become obvious. He had read a great deal of the writings of Karl Marx as well Bertrand Russell and Anatole France. So deeply was he influenced by his reading that he gave up luxuries and began sleeping on the floor. In 1927 he left for Oxford to complete his undergraduate studies. There, he was further influenced by Marxist philosophy. In 1927, he contracted tuberculosis and was sent to a sanatorium in Switzerland. It was during this time that he read a great deal of French and Russian literature and books on Communism. It was here that he saw his first Russian film, too. By the time he returned to Oxford in 1928 he was a confirmed Marxist.

For Zahir, anti-capitalism went hand in hand with anti-imperialism and, in 1929, he was even assaulted by the police in London for being a part of a peaceful procession against the Simon Commission. He started the newspaper *Bharat* in 1930 with the help of some friends. After finishing his studies at Oxford he travelled through Germany, Italy, Denmark and Austria on his journey back to India in 1932. At the end of this year, he published *Angarey* at his private expense.

Soon after, he left for England to finish studying law at

Angarey

Lincoln's Inn. In 1935, Sajjad Zahir and novelist Mulk Raj Anand went to Paris to attend the International Conference for Defense of Culture which had been organized by André Gide, Henri Barbusse and Andre Malraux to protest the rise of fascism across Europe.[11] Luminaries such as E. M. Forster, Aldous Huxley, Elya Ehrenberg, Boris Pasternak, Anna Seghers and Ernest Toller, all of whom were attending the conference, deeply impressed the two Indians and they decided to strengthen the association they had founded. A year later, the concerted efforts of a group of like-minded persons found its culmination in the first conference of the IPWA held on 9 and 10 April 1936. Popularly known as Anjuman Tarraqi Pasand Mussanafin in Urdu and Akhil Bharatiya Pragatisheel Lekhak Sangh in Hindi, the group was united by the common vision of using writing as a means of attacking class and gender discrimination in an effort to usher in an egalitarian social order.

Sajjad Zahir continued to be deeply involved both in politics and literature through his life. He became Uttar Pradesh state secretary of the Communist Party of India (CPI) as well as a member of the working committee of the Congress in 1936. He was nominated in-charge of the Delhi branch of the CPI in 1939. He was jailed for two years during the Second World War for opposing Indian participation in it. After his release in 1942, he became the editor of the CPI newspaper *Qaumi Jung* in Bombay. The

---

[11] Ibid.

Introduction

account of his arrest—along with the revolutionary poet, Faiz Ahmad Faiz—in Pakistan for his alleged involvement with the so-called 'Rawalpindi Conspiracy Case' in 1951 reads stranger than any fiction. Sajjad Zahir also edited the CPI Urdu weekly *Hayat* for many years. *Zahir was* a fairly prolific writer, and a list of his major works is as follows:

- *Angarey* (Nizami Press, Lucknow, 1932)
- *Beemaar* (Jamia Press, Delhi)
- *London ki Ek Raat* (Halqaye-e-adab, Lucknow, 1942)
- *Urdu, Hindi, Hindustani* (Kutab Publishers, Bombay, 1947)
- *Letters: Naquoosh-e-Zindaan* (Maktaba Shahrah, Delhi, 1951)
- *Zikr-e-Hafiz* (Anjuman Tarraqui-e Urdu, Aligarh, 1956)
- *Roshnai* (Maktaba Urdu, Lahore, 1956)
- *Pighla Neelam* (Nai Roshani Prakashan, Delhi, 1964)
- *Meri Suno* (Star Publishers, Delhi, 1967)
- *Mazzamein-e-Sajjad Zaheer* (published posthumously by the UP Urdu Academy, Lucknow, 1979)

Sajjad Zahir died on 13 September 1973.

Ahmed Ali (1910-1993) was born in Delhi and educated at the Universities of Aligarh and Lucknow. A brilliant student, he received a first-class honours degree and, after completing his M.A., began teaching English at Lucknow University. Ahmed Ali taught English in China before the

Angarey

revolution and, besides this, he was also a visiting professor at several American universities. Ahmed Ali became an officer of the foreign service of Pakistan after Partition and served as Pakistan's ambassador to Morocco for a while.

Ahmed Ali's first poem, 'The Lake of Dreams', written in English, was published in 1926 in the Aligarh University magazine. His novel, *Twilight in Delhi*, was praised by E. M Forster in his preface to the first edition of his novel, *A Passage to India*. This was followed by:

- Two stories in *Angarey* (1932)
- *Sholay* (1934)
- *Hamari Gali* (1942)
- *Qaidkhana* (1944)
- *Maut se Pehle* (1945)
- *Twilight in Delhi* (1942)

After he went to Pakistan, Ahmed Ali wrote two novels, *Ocean of Night* (1965) and *Of Rats and Diplomats* (1985). His English translation of the *Quran Sharif* was published in 1984.

Disagreements regarding concepts, ideas and praxis in a group of highly gifted and zealous young individuals is to be expected. And this is exactly what happened between the four writers. Ahmed Ali broke away from the group in around 1938. In an interview with Carlo Coppola, Ahmed Ali states that his reason for doing so was his reluctance to accept the close identification between socialist realism and progressive writing that he felt had begun to gradually dominate the group. Nonetheless, he emphasizes that this

Introduction

aesthetic departure from the group did not in any way imply for him a divorce from progressive writing itself. However, Sajjad Zahir, in his in book *Roshnai*, puts down Ahmed Ali's extreme sensitivity and personal ego as being the reasons for his departure. The real truth about this may probably never be fully known.

Popularly known as 'Angarewali', Dr **Rashid Jahan** (1905-1952) was targeted much more viciously than the other writers of *Angarey* . She was pilloried not only for her defiance of existing norms but for doing so despite being a woman. The criticism, however, only strengthened her resolve.

Born to Shaikh Muhammad Abdullah and Waheeda Begum, Rashid Jahan inherited her passion for reform from her parents who devoted their lives to the cause of education, especially that of women. A Kashmiri Brahmin by birth, Shaikh Muhammad Abdullah converted to Islam and was an ardent admirer of Sir Syed Ahmad Khan. The first school that Rashid Jahan attended was the school for girls which had been founded by her parents in 1906. She finished her matriculation in 1922 from Lucknow and joined the Lady Hardinge Medical College in Delhi as a student. This provided her with the opportunity of seeing the physical and mental subjugation of a large cross-section of women at close quarters. Her condemnation of their painful situations is reflected in her writings, including the short story and play which she contributed to *Angarey.*

A committed member of the CPI, Rashid Jahan was

a writer, an activist, a doctor and a lot more. She was an advocate for the oppressed as well as a dynamic member of the Indian People's Theatre Association (IPTA). Rashid Jahan was also one of the founder-members of the PWA. She continued to write—mostly short stories and plays—throughout her life. Her published works are scattered in various collections and it is only in the recent past that some scholars have begun to diligently pull them together and bring them to the reading public. Some of her writings have been published in the following collections:

- *Aurat aur Dusre Afsane wa Drame* (1937)
- *Shola-e-jwala* (1952)
- *Woh aur Dusre Afsane wa Drame* (1977)

The memoirs of Rashid Jahan's sister, Khurshid Mirza, *A Woman of Substance: The Memoirs of Begum Khurshid Mirza* (2005) too has a chapter on her.

Rashid Jahan married Mahmuduzzafar in 1934. The extraordinary life of Rashid Jahan came to an anguished, abrupt end. Diagnosed with uterine cancer, she had gone for treatment to Moscow where she breathed her last and was buried in a cemetery there. Rashid Jahan was just forty-seven then, and was at the height of her activism-related work and at the peak of her creative powers.

Mahmuduzzafar (1908-1954) was the son of Sahibzada Saiduzzafar Khan, a medical doctor and the head of Lucknow Medical College. He was sent at the age of twelve to study

Introduction

at the Sherborne School in Dorset from where he went to Balliol College, Oxford, to study economics.[12] It was here that he was first exposed to Marxism. Nonetheless, the long years of absence from India seemed to have had no effect when he returned to India after finishing his studies. Mahmuduzzafar went on to become a devoted member of the CPI and remained an active member of the PWA throughout his life. Soon after his marriage with Rashid Jahan, Mahmuduzzafar joined the Mohammadan Anglo-Oriental College, Amritsar, as its vice-principal and taught English and History there. After spending about three years in Amritsar, Mahmuduzzafar decided to become a full-time worker of the CPI. His biggest regret on his return to India seems to have been his unfamiliarity with the Urdu language. Consequently, he did not publish much in Urdu and the only well-known book by Mahmuduzzafar that seems to be in existence is *A Quest for Life*—a travelogue about his time in Russia.

Mahmuduzzafar has one story in *Angarey*. The story, titled 'Jawanmardi' (Masculinity), was originally written in English and then translated into Urdu by Sajjad Zahir.

All four contributors to *Angarey* belonged to middle-class or upper-middle-class families and were exposed to contemporary Western thought, literature and ideas. They had

---

[12] Carlo Coppola, p. 58.

Angarey

located themselves within the matrix of conflicting worldviews which included the attempt to usher in egalitarianism, liberalism and individualism against the rising tide of fascism. The vision of a classless and oppressionless society, free from religious and social dogmas, gender and class oppression and political subjugation is what fired up their writing. It was this range of highly incongruent influences which actually prepared the ground in which the seed of protest-through-literature could be sown.

The collection as a whole, as well as the stories and the play independently, quite clearly highlight the commonality of vision of the four contributors regarding the content, form and idiom of writing, the role of the writer, as well as the relationship between literature and society. In fact, *Angarey* may be seen as an articulation of the belief in an organic connection between aesthetic expression and socio-cultural and political processes. The collection becomes symbolic of the agency that its writers had bestowed upon themselves in highlighting the underlying relations between the innermost workings of an individual's mind and external socio-historical forces.

This redefinition of subject, form and language reveals a clear impact of Western literature. The influence of nineteenth-century French writers like Gustave Flaubert and Honore de Balzac is visible in the rejection of all forms of embellishment or escapism in *Angarey* which represents characters as a creation of their social environments. Also visible is the influence of late nineteenth and early twentieth

Introduction

century philosophers and psychologists such as Henri Bergson and William James who hotly contested the nature of human experience and the human psyche within the framework of the multiplicity of time. The recognition of the coexistence of several paradoxical features like external clock time along with subjective or mental time; the past and the present; impromptu shifts between elation and despair; and the unpredictability of remembrance and forgetfulness, led to the imagining of the human psyche as an infinite continuum. In her well-known statement regarding this concept, Virginia Woolf states, 'Life is not a series of gig lamps symmetrically arranged; life is a luminous halo, a semi-transparent envelope surrounding us from the beginning of consciousness to the end.' It is the 'flickering of that innermost flame which flashes its messages through the brain' that novelists like Virginia Woolf and James Joyce attempt to 'preserve' and communicate through the use of narrative techniques like the stream of consciousness and the interior monologue. The representation of life as being a complex continuum in fiction needed not just an innovative narrative technique but also an equally new form to communicate this ephemeral reality that refused 'to be contained any longer in such ill-fitting vestments' that provided 'a plot ... comedy, tragedy, love interest, and an air of probability embalming the whole'.[13]

---

[13] All the quotes regarding content, technique and form of modern fiction have been taken from Virginia Woolf, 'The Common Reader'

Angarey

The stories in *Angarey* translate many of these literary doctrines into practice. Critics like Linda Wentick have discussed how *Angarey* may be seen as 'an important initial step in the evolution of modernist fiction in Urdu'.[14] The stream of consciousness, the interior monologue, and the breakdown of conventional punctuation are some of the techniques that the contributors of the collection use to represent the ebb and flow of human consciousness. These techniques are combined with a severe indictment of colonial authority, political suppression, social iniquity and religious hypocrisy. The writers thus simultaneously enter the mental world of the characters, preoccupy themselves with their sordid and foetid physical world, quite like the naturalists and, at the same time, possess a kind of detached objectivity which enables them to record impressions and experiences at specific moments.

Sajjad Zahir's 'Insomnia', 'The Same Uproar, Once Again' and Ahmed Ali's 'A Night of Mahavatt, the Winter Rain' trace the floundering thoughts of characters struggling to come to terms with their deprivation. 'The Clouds Don't Come' by Ahmed Ali and 'Heaven Assured!' by Sajjad Zahir present, among other things, a strong condemnation of religious duplicity. Sajjad Zahir in 'Dulari' brings

---

from Andrew McNeille (ed.) *The Essays of Virginia Woolf, Volume 4: 1925-1928* (London: The Hogarth Press, 1984), pp. 157-164.
[14]As quoted by Bodh Prakash, *Writing Partition: Aesthetics and Ideology in Hindi and Urdu Literature* (Delhi: Pearson Education India, 2009) p.9.

Introduction

together the issues of class discrimination and gender. Mahmuduzzafar hits out at the severe patriarchal oppression of women in 'Masculinity'. Rashid Jahan's story 'A Trip to Delhi', told in flashback, explores the same issue. Her play 'Behind the Veil' articulates the various ways in which patriarchy and socio-religious codes manipulate to control the woman's mind and body.

Thus, it was the search for a dynamic interpretation of life through literature, co-existing with the vision of literature as a means of changing society, which led to the establishment of the Indian Progressive Writers' Association (IPWA) in London on 24 November 1934. IPWA subsequently matured into the Progressive Writers' Association which, ultimately, forged a new literary consciousness.

Angarey and the Progressive Writers' Association

In April 1933, Mahmuduzzafar had called for an association of progressive writers to be formed with his article 'In Defence of Angarey'. Besides this, the journal *Seep*, published from Karachi, carried Ahmed Ali's article titled 'Taraqqui Pasand Tehreek Aur Takhleequi Musannif' in which he writes,'Mahmuduzzafar, on Rashid Jahan's as well as my suggestion, announced the formation of the "League of Progressive Authors" in 1933. Since Sajjad Zahir was in London, Mahmuduzzafar undertook the responsibility of securing his consent. Sajjad Zahir later sent his consent note by post. In 1932-33, the chief purpose of the writers was

Angarey

purely literary and the only political aspect of the endeavour was to achieve the right to freely criticize the problems of human society in general and, specifically, of the Indian sub-continent.'

During his stay in Europe, Sajjad Zahir attended the World Conference of the Writers for the Defense of Culture in Paris. He was deeply influenced by the conference and after his return to India in 1935, Zakir began informal discussions with writers like Firaq Gorakhpuri, Ahetesham Hussain, Shivdan Singh Chauhan, Amar Nath Jha and Tara Chand regarding the establishment of the Anjuman Taraqqui Pasand Musannifin (Progressive Writers' Association) and even got their signatures expressing support.

It so happened that Tara Chand had organized a conference of Hindi and Urdu writers in Allahabad under the aegis of 'Hindustani Academy' in Allahabad. Writers such as Premchand, Josh Malihabadi, Abdul Haq and Daya Narain Nigam were in Allahabad to attend the conference. Sajjad Zahir, too, decided to attend and it was here that he was introduced to Premchand by Firaq Gorakhpuri for the first time.[15] Within a few days, Sajjad Zahir invited several writers like Premchand, Josh, Abdul Haq and Daya Narain Nigam for breakfast, where he got these writers to sign and support the manifesto he had prepared.

It was also decided that the first conference of the

---

[15] A. A. Fatami, *Taraqqui Pasand Tehreek* (Karachi: Pakistan Publishing House, 2011) pp. 37-38.

Introduction

PWA would be held in Lucknow, with Premchand as the chairman. In a letter written on 5 March 1936, Premchand expressed some hesitation and suggested that someone else like K. M. Munshi, Zakir Hussain or Jawaharlal Nehru be selected to chair the first session of the PWA. However, he finally agreed after some persuasion. It was as chairman of this conference that Premchand delivered his famous talk 'Sahitya ka Uddeshya' in which, amongst other ideas, he expressed the pressing need to bring about a transformation in the concept of beauty in literature. It was here that he also articulated the connection between politics and literature by describing literature as being the light that does not follow but leads politics.[16]

Discussing the immense significance of the PWA on literatures in India, noted scholar and critic Namvar Singh says, 'Sajjad Zahir in 1936 started the PWA with a handful of writers. If we look at it carefully, then we find that this actually changed the ethos of literature. This was true not just for Urdu but for all other languages, too. The histories of languages like Hindi, Bangla, Tamil Gujarati and Marathi reveal that after 1936, there was a major shift in their literatures. Before this, farmers, labourers, as well as the poor and the common people, were not considered fit subjects for literature. Though Premchand did initiate this trend of representing the common person, the post-1936 period saw the surging of a new wave. Not just Urdu shayari

---

[16]Ibid. p. 46.

Angarey

(poetry) but the tone of even poets like Nirala underwent a change. The timbre of Pant, Mahadevi Verma and Dinkar changed too. This is also the time when Yashpal entered the literary scene with his stories and novels. A whole army had congregated.'[17]

Angarey: The Journey Home

Five copies of *Angarey* escaped the blaze in 1933. However, their owners did not wish to be identified. As a consequence, it was impossible to find even a single copy of the collection. It was only in 1987 that the microfilm of the book was found to have been preserved in the British Museum in London. This was the starting point of *Angarey*'s journey home. Qamar Rais, the head of the Urdu department of Delhi University at that time, was instrumental in having the microfilm brought to India. The stories were then edited by Khalid Alvi who added a long and well-researched introduction to it. The book was published as *Angarey* in Urdu by Educational Publishing House, Delhi, in 1995. The collection evoked a phenomenal response and has run into several editions since it was first published.

The Urdu edition brought together by Khalid Alvi is the original source text for this English translation. In addition, his insightful and exhaustive introduction to the book has provided rich and valuable material for the study and analysis

---

[17] A. A. Fatmi, *Taraqqi Pasand Tehrir*, Karachi, p.129.

Introduction

of the various complex issues surrounding the writers, the creation, the controversy and the exciting journey of *Angarey* as well as its legacy.

Notes on the Translation

Every book is unique for its textual features as well as the contextual framework within which it is conceived, produced and communicated. The present translation, too, has some singular features. It was one of the many free-wheeling conversations—a regular feature of Zakir Husain Delhi College (ZHDC)—which actually engendered the idea of the book. The oldest college of the University of Delhi, ZHDC has the largest number of language departments in the university and having taught in the college for more than two decades, I'm no stranger to the easy interaction of language and language cultures that happen quite spontaneously in the staff room.

It was one such chat with my colleague Khalid Alvi regarding Rashid Jahan which led to a discussion on *Angarey*. I had come to know a few facts about Rashid Jahan at a small poetry reading event the day before. That little information whetted my appetite for more. And who better than Khalid-sa'ab to have answered my queries. I have known him as a person who wears his scholarship with consummate ease. One has to only find the opportunity of discussing Urdu literature with him to discover his serious interest and scholarship in the discipline. The day I mentioned Rashid Jahan to him

Angarey

was one such day. It was only after he started talking about Rashid Jahan and her comrades in literature that I realized that he was the editor of the Urdu edition of *Angarey* which was re-published in 1995.

The idea of translating *Angarey* into English began to take shape when I found out that Khalid-sa'ab had, many years ago, transcribed six stories from the collection into Devanagari. These were 'Jannat ki Basharat', 'Phir Yeh Hungama', 'Garmiyon ki Ek Raat', 'Neend Nahin Aati', 'Dulari' and 'Badal Nahin Aate'. He had done this with the idea of bringing out a Hindi translation of *Angarey* but it somehow remained incomplete. He handed these scripts to me. I was fascinated by what I read and wanted more. The only way this could have happened was by Khalid-sa'ab reading the stories aloud to me. He agreed to do so and I decided to directly translate the stories into English as he read them out to me.

The reading room for teachers in our college library was the space that became a witness to the process of translation where languages, scripts, orality and the written word began to slip in and out of their encoded locations. There was very little in the reading of the original Urdu—including many culture-specific references—that I could not comprehend and grasp. It was a clear revelation of a living multi-linguality that surrounds us through our ordinary, routine lives. We soak up and internalize many different languages and cultures that live around us rather unconsciously and often end up knowing more languages than we give ourselves credit

Introduction

for. The oral proximity of languages like Hindustani and Urdu, however, fades away when we approach the written scripts which are entirely different from each other. The apparent ease of translating from speech to the written word is overtaken by the impediment of an unfamiliar script and we realize how important schooling and instruction are to even begin to get familiar with the scripts of languages that we learn informally during the process of societal interaction. It is in such situations that I believe, what may be called 'collaborative translation' becomes extremely valuable since it allows the active pooling in of language resources of persons other than the sole translator. The large number of language varieties and the proximity or distance between them makes it impossible for even serious scholars to master many languages. However, in the event of an overlap between the language, the literature and the culture of the source and the target languages such coordinated/collaborative translation can prove to be fruitful.

The selection of what is considered the most suitable word or phrase from various options available to us is one that is conditioned by our personal perception as well as the theoretical appreciation of the process and the outcome of translation. The process of linguistic, textual and cultural translation inevitably embraces issues like equivalence, 'foreignizing' and/or treating culture as the basic, functioning unit of the translation process. My personal theoretical conviction tilts towards that of Susan Bassnett and Andrè Lefevere who see the possibility of

Angarey

re-approachment between cultural studies and translation studies. It is for this reason that words like 'moulvi', 'aadaab', 'mujra' and 'chaprasi' have been left in their original form in this translation, especially in instances where the meaning or implication of the word is clear from the context itself.

The allusions and metaphors were more difficult to deal with. I have tried to convey the sense of these allusions and metaphors within the main body of the text itself. However, I had little choice but to resort to notes where these began to sound awkward.

An additional challenge was the translation of poetry, mostly couplets written by well-known Urdu poets. The gist of the poetry in prose follows the quotes in most cases, especially if its significance is evident through its placement in the text. I decided to include notes wherever I felt that a couplet needed a detailed gloss.

The text is also interspersed with many Quranic references which impart a historical as well as scholarly density to it. Most of these allusions were explicated in great detail by Khalid-sa'ab. I also tried to read and research some of these on my own and have tried to convey their essence to the reader to the best of my ability. I'm certain that these are far from perfect and I take the entire responsibility for any deficiencies whatsoever.

—Vibha S. Chauhan

Introduction

I have been involved with Urdu literature and language for as long as I can remember. My formal education and systemized training in the language is more or less an extension of my life-long passion. The history, evolution and various forms of expression in the language have always held immense fascination for me. This has been reinforced by the good fortune of having friends who have shared their knowledge with me through stimulating discussions—which have been sometimes informal and, at other times, highly academic and formal—leaving no genre of Urdu literature untouched. What, however, continued to happen rather frequently is the repeated mention of the collection *Angarey* and its influence on the growth and shaping of the Urdu short story. Despite its obviously significant place in the literary and social history of the Urdu short story and its close connection with literature, culture, reform and protest, none of us had read the text of *Angarey* in its entirety. Some of us had been able to lay our hands on some part of it or the other but the complete text seemed to be completely out of bounds. It was available neither in libraries nor in private collections. Qamar Rais, my senior, friend, and a serious scholar, whetted our appetite for *Angarey* with his article 'Urdu Mein *Angarey* ki Ravayat'. Besides this, the use of the stream-of-consciousness technique in *Angarey* was seen by some critics as having a major influence on works like *Aag ka Dariya* by Qurratulain Haider. In short, all this led to my resolve of working towards bringing out the entire text of *Angarey*. Like many earlier occasions I found unstinted

Angarey

support from Qamar Rais. With some effort we found the microfilm of *Angarey* in the British Museum in London and soon managed to have the complete text with us.

My work on *Angarey* began in 1987 and it was many years later that the compilation of the original Urdu *Angarey* was published in Delhi in 1995. I had decided to provide as exhaustive and detailed information as possible about the context of the collection. I travelled to several cities like Lucknow and libraries like the Raza Library in Rampur and Madina Manzil in Bijnore to trace journals, newspapers, articles and books from 1932 onwards which could throw some light on the events connected with the publication and banning of *Angarey*. I found the bi-weekly newspaper *Madina* as well as some other extremely important old documents in Madina Manzil in Bijnore.

My compilation of the nine stories and the play which comprise *Angarey* has its roots in a genuine search for what I believe has been one of the most significant but neglected texts in not just Urdu literature, but in the literature of India on the whole. I am deeply grateful to Nikhat Kazmi for her article '*Angarey* Rekindled Again' which was published in the *Times of India* where she worked at that time. I was also soon to discover that the compilation had given me a new name and identity, not just in India but also in Pakistan. I visited Pakistan in 2007 where I went to bookshops in Urdu Bazar in Lahore. I had a local friend who introduced me to a bookseller by my name. The bookseller, however, immediately identified me as 'Angarewale' Khalid Alvi. At

Introduction

another time, while walking across Peshawar University with my friend Ibn-e-Kawal, I met Mateen Ahmed, a young lecturer in a college in Peshawar University. He wanted to discuss my compilation of *Angarey* which had been was made compulsory reading by his PhD supervisor.

The interest that was generated by this book led me feel that it should be translated in Hindi and go to a wider readership. It was with that in mind that I transcribed six stories of the collection into Devnagari. This work however, could never be completed and it was only now after many years that by sheer chance my colleague and friend Vibha and I began to discuss the book and decided to translate it into English.

The translation, though not easy, has been an extremely rewarding experience for us. I hope you will enjoy reading *Angarey* as much as we enjoyed translating it.

—Khalid Alvi

A Summer Night
~ Sajjad Zahir ~

After offering the namaaz of Esha, the last prayer of the night, Munshi Barkat Ali went out for a stroll and soon found himself in Ameenabad. It was a breezeless summer night. People were standing around sherbet stalls, chatting. Some boys selling newspapers screamed at the top of their voices. Hawkers selling jasmine garlands pursued and pestered the gentlemen walking around. The tonga-wallas and the rickshaw-wallas called out for passengers without pause.

'Chowk! One passenger for Chowk! Mian, should I take you to Chowk?'

'Huzoor! Do you need a tonga?'

'Jasmine garlands!'

'Do you have sweet, frozen cream?'

Munshiji bought a garland, drank some sherbet, popped

Angarey

a paan into his mouth, and stepped into a park. The benches there were all occupied. Many people were stretched out on the grass. Some people with a zest for music but with no ear for it were creating a racket. Others just sat quietly. They had pulled up their dhotis and were absorbed in scratching their legs and thighs, and suddenly springing up and swatting at the mosquitoes which settled on them. Munshiji always wore pyjamas and was naturally angered by this uncouthness. He quietly said to himself, 'These wretched people will always remain uncultured! They will never learn.'

Just then, somebody called out loudly from a bench nearby, 'Munshi Barkat Ali.'

Munshiji turned around.

'Aha! Lalaji, it's you. So, all well I hope?'

Lalaji was the head clerk in the office where Munshiji worked. Munshiji was his subordinate. Having taken off his shoes, Lalaji had placed his obese body in the middle of the bench and looked well settled with his feet pulled up under him. He lovingly caressed his paunch as he continued to talk in a loud voice to his two companions who sat very respectfully on the two opposite ends of the bench. Having spotted Munshiji, Lalaji had called out to him, too. Munshiji stood in front of him.

Lalaji laughed. 'So, Munshi Barkat Ali, I see that you've bought these garlands and things. What are your intentions?' He broke into boisterous laughter and looked towards his two companions for appreciation. They understood what Lalaji was hinting at and obligingly laughed.

A Summer Night

Munshiji, too, smiled weakly and said, 'What intentions and hopes can I afford to nurse? You know too well what a poor man I am. One can hardly breathe because of the heat. It has become impossible to sleep at nights. I just bought this garland hoping that it might bring some sleep.'

Lalaji ran his palm over his bald head, laughed, and said, 'You sure are stylish, Munshi, and why shouldn't you be?' Having said this, he went back to conversing with his two companions.

Munshiji judged that to be his moment to slip away. 'So then, Lalaji,' he said, 'I must leave now. Aadaab,' and walked ahead. In his heart, he cursed this meeting with the wretched Lala. It had ruined his evening. Wasn't it enough that he spent the whole day dealing with his whims? And to top it, he wants to know what my intentions are! Am I some rich landlord that I would make the rounds of the kothas enjoying mujras? Do I ever have more than fifty paise in my pocket? A wife and family, sixty rupees a month, and the income from the kickbacks so uncertain. It was a lucky coincidence that I managed to earn one rupee today. These rustics are becoming cunning and well informed about official matters these days. It is only after hours of cajoling and wheedling that they fish out even a mere paisa from their pockets. Then they behave as if they are our masters and refuse us even the basic courtesies. These vulgar, low people! They have all gone mad. It is the white-collared people like us who are in deep trouble. On the one hand are these uncouth people who now think no end of themselves. And, on the other,

Angarey

the government and the bosses who are getting stricter by the day. Just recently, barely two months ago in Benares, two clerks—the poor things—were dismissed for accepting bribes. That's what always happens. The helpless, poor people are the ones who get squeezed. The high-ranking officers just get transferred from one place to another, if at all.

Someone called out from close by, 'Munshiji, sahib.' It was Jumman, the peon.

'Aha! So it's you Jumman.'

However, even after acknowledging Jumman, Munshiji kept walking. He turned away from the park and reached Nazeerabad. Jumman tagged along. Munshiji—short and slim, with a boat-shaped velvet cap on his head and a garland in hand—walked in front and just a couple of steps behind him strode the tall and burly peon, Jumman, wearing a turban on his head.

Munshiji began to speculate about why Jumman was trailing him. So, Jumman! How's everything? I just met head-clerk sahib in the park. He, too, was complaining about the heat.'

'Aji Munshiji, what can I say? Heat is not the only thing that's killing us. I left office only at about four-thirty or five. After that I had to mark my attendance at the boss' house. Only now have I been relieved and allowed to go home. You can surely understand how, from ten in the morning to eight o'clock at night, I run from pillar to post all day. After working in the court, I must run to and from the market at least thrice. From there I buy and carry

A Summer Night

back things like ice, vegetables, fruits and, as if that were not enough, I get scolded too. "Why did you pay an extra paisa? Why are the fruits rotten?" Begum sahiba didn't like the mangoes I bought today and ordered me to return them. I said, "Huzoor, how can I return these at this time in the night?" She only said, "I don't care. I don't want to buy garbage." And so huzoor I was stuck with mangoes worth one rupee. I went back to the fruit-seller but I can't even begin to describe how much I had to squabble with him. He finally paid back twelve annas for mangoes costing one rupee and I had to lose a chavanni on the deal. These are the last few days of the month and I swear huzoor, there is not even a morsel of food in the house. I just don't what to do. How will I go home and face my wife?'

Munshiji was getting alarmed by the peon's account. After all, why should Jumman recount his whole story to him? Who doesn't know that the poor have their troubles, their scarcities and their hunger? But Munshiji was not responsible for it all. His own life was far from luxurious. Quite inadvertently, Munshiji's hand moved to his pocket. The rupee—the kickback he had received that day—was in his pocket, safe and sound.

'You are right, mian Jumman! The poor hardly have any way out these days. Anybody you meet complains that there is no food in the house. Actually, if you ask me, all these are clear indications that the Day of Judgement is close at hand. All the scoundrels are having a good time and the virtuous and the devout are suffering.'

Angarey

Jumman listened quietly to what Munshiji had to say and kept following him. Munshiji continued to talk but his anxiety was growing. He couldn't be sure if his words were making any impression at all on Jumman.

'Yesterday, after the Jumma namaaz, Maulana-sahib's religious discourse listed the warning signs which herald the Day of Judgement. Mian Jumman, believe me, everybody who heard it was in tears. All this is actually the consequence of our sins, brother. Is there any flaw or villainy that we are free from? And so, any chastisement that God has determined for us cannot be an adequate sentence for us. Allah inflicted far more severe punishment on Bani Israel for deeds that were much less wicked. One's hair stands on end at the mere thought of those tortures. You, of course, must be already aware of all this.'

Jumman responded, 'We are poor people, Munshiji. How can we of these things? I have heard about the Day of Judgement but huzoor, who was this poor creature Bani Israel?'

Munshiji was a little comforted by this query. The conversation had moved away from poverty and on to the Day of Judgement and Bani Israel. While Munshiji did not know much about the community, he could still speak and deliberate upon it for hours.

'Really! Wah mian Jumman, wah! You call yourself a Muslim and don't know who Bani Israel was? All our religious discourses are full of allusions to Bani Israel. I hope that you have at least heard the name of Hazrat Moosa Kaleemullah?'

'Ji? What did you say? Kaleemullah?'

A Summer Night

'Arre bhai, Hazrat Moosa, Moo ... sa.'

'Moosa ... Is he the same one who was struck by lightning?'

Munshiji burst out laughing—he was quite relaxed by now. They had almost reached the Kaiserbagh crossroads. There, certainly, he would be able to get rid of this greedy peon. It is not very pleasant to be trailed by a penniless man—that, too, a man one knows—when one has come out for a stroll, hoping for some relaxation and peace, after having offered namaaz and eaten dinner. But what could Munshiji have done? He could not have kicked Jumman away like a dog. After all, they worked together in the same court of law every day and, to add to his woes, the peon was an unrefined man from the lower classes. If he became offensive or rude by any chance, then Munshiji's hard-earned reputation would be publicly sullied. It would be better to walk up to the crossroads and take the other road home. It was the best way to get rid of him.

'Anyway!' Munshiji began with finality, 'I will tell you about Bani Israel and Moosa some other day. Right now, I have to go that way for some work. Salaam, mian Jumman.'

Munshiji then began to walk swiftly towards the cinema in Kaiserbagh. When he saw Munshiji speed away, Jumman froze for a moment. He was bewildered and could not decide what to do next. Sweat beaded his forehead and his gaze wandered around aimlessly. He could see the bright electric lights, the fountain, cinema posters, the hotel, shops, cars, tongas, ikkas and, high up above everything else, the sky and

Angarey

the glittering stars—in short, God's entire province.

The very next moment, however, Jumman bounded behind Munshiji who was looking at the cinema posters, pleased to have gotten away from Jumman.

Jumman went up close to him and said, 'Munshiji!'

Munshiji's heart missed a beat. All that conversation about religion, the talk about the Day of Judgement—all that had proved to be in vain. Munshiji did not respond.

'Munshiji,' Jumman said, 'if you could loan me just one rupee, I would always be...'

Munshiji turned around and said, 'Mian Jumman, I know that you are hard up but you know my condition very well. Let alone a rupee, I won't be able to lend you even a single paisa. Do you think I would have hidden it from you if I had it? If I had any money at all, I would have given it to you even without your asking me for it.'

Jumman, however, started pleading. 'Munshiji, I give you my word. I'll return it as soon as I get my salary. The truth is that there is nobody else who can help me...'

Munshiji was usually extremely discomfited by this kind of pestering. And any refusal—even though genuine—is always painful to accept. Which is why he had hoped to avoid this situation from the start.

The film show ended just then and the audience walked out.

Someone called out from close by, 'Arre mian Barkat, how come you're here?' Munshiji turned away from Jumman to face a plump man, about thirty or thirty-five years old. The man was wearing an angarkha and a dopalli cap. He was chewing a paan and smoking a cigarette.

Munshi said, 'Aha! It's you! I am seeing you after years. You've abandoned Lucknow completely. Or who knows, you may be visiting often, but why would you be interested in meeting poor people like us?'

The man was an old friend of Munshiji's from college. He was also fairly wealthy. Munshiji's friend said, 'Forget about all that. I am in Lucknow only for two days. I've come to have fun, some entertainment. Come along with me and we'll attend such a mujra that you will remember it for all time to come. Don't think about it too much. I have my car right here, just come along. Have you ever heard Noorjehan sing? Ah! What singing! What expression! What dancing! The grace! The elegance! Her supple waist! The tinkling of her ankle-bells! The recital will happen in my courtyard and will conclude only once Noorjehan has sung the raga Bhairavi at dawn. Don't think about over it too much now, just come along. Anyway, tomorrow is a Sunday. Your wife! Are you scared of being beaten up by Begum-sahiba? What's the point of marrying if you end up becoming a woman's slave? Come along, mian, come along now! Pacifying the sulking begum has its own delights...'

An old friend, a car ride, music, dancing, Noorjehan's heavenly eyes, her polished tete-a-tetes—Munshiji leapt into the car. Jumman did not figure in his thoughts at all. But, as the car pulled away, he saw Jumman silent and immobile, rooted to the same spot.

Dulari

~ Sajjad Zahir ~

Though she had lived and grown up in the house, the londi was in her sixteenth or seventeenth year when she finally ran away. Nobody knew who her parents were. Her universe had been limited to this house and its inhabitants. Sheikh Nazim Ali-sahib was a prosperous man. WIth God's grace, the family had been blessed with many sons and daughters. Begum-sahiba, too, was alive and active, and the absolute sovereign of the women's quarters. Dulari served Begum-sahiba exclusively. Other maids—including the ones who had been especially employed to take care of the children—were often engaged in household chores, too. They would work for a month or two, or even one or two years, and would then quit after some or the other quarrel over some minor issue or the other. But, as far Dulari was concerned, this was the only refuge she had. The family

Dulari

members were quite kind to her—after all, the people from the higher classes always take care of the ones from the lower classes! Dulari had no complaints about food or clothes and, compared to the other maidservants, she was much better off. But despite this, if she ever had any argument with the other maids, she was always mocked. 'I am not a londi like you,' they would say. Dulari would have no reply.

Her childhood had been untroubled and carefree. She was born into a class that was inferior not just to the bibis, the women in the family, but even to the maidservants. This was God's design. He is the one who determines who should be esteemed and who humiliated. What was the point of grumbling about it all? Dulari, too, did not complain about the poverty. But as childhood departed and made way for youth, and the dim, unfamiliar restlessness which sometimes brings bitterness and, at other times, delight into life, she was often depressed. This was, however, an internal state of mind about which she neither knew the cause nor the remedy for it. The choti sahibzaadi of the family, Haseena-begum, and Dulari were of about the same age and used to play together. But as they grew older, the distance between them widened with each passing year. Choti sahibzaadi was from a respectable family; her time was well utilized in reading, writing and stitching. Dulari would dust the rooms, do the dishes, fill up and store water for use. She was beautiful. Nature had gifted her with long limbs and a rounded, curvy body, but her clothes were usually filthy and her body smelled bad. Of course, on festive days or on those occasions when

Angarey

she went out with Begum-sahiba or the young girls of the family, she wore her special clothes, washed herself and adorned her face.

※

That Shab-e-barat, which falls fifteen days before Ramzan, Dulari looked like a doll. The women's courtyard was ablaze with fireworks. All the family members as well the domestic helps were watching the show. The elder son, bade sahibzaade Kazim, was also present. Kazim was about twenty-one years old and was about to finish college. While Begum-sahiba was exceedingly fond of him, Kazim seemed to be perennially exasperated with his family—he considered them to be too conservative and unsophisticated. When he came home for vacations, he spent all his time arguing with them. And while he was generally critical of traditional customs and rituals, he would first express his disagreement but would then come around to put up with them. He was unwilling to go much beyond expressing his difference of opinion.

He put his head on his mother's shoulder and said, 'Ammi-jaan! I'm thirsty.'

Begum-sahiba's response was brimming with love. 'Have some sherbet, my son,' she said, 'I will ask somebody to get it.' She then called Dulari in and asked her to prepare some for her son.

But Kazim said, 'No, Ammi-jaan. Let her watch the show. I will go inside and help myself.' Dulari, however, having received the command, was walking towards the inner rooms. Kazim followed her. Dulari was trying to decide which sherbet bottle to pick out from the dark, tiny store when Kazim reached.

Dulari turned around to ask, 'Which sherbet should I prepare for you?' But she received no answer. Kazim gazed intently at Dulari. Her body began to tremble and her eyes filled with tears. She picked up a bottle and walked towards the door. Kazim cut across in front of her, took the bottle from her hand, put it away, and then embraced her. She shut her eyes and handed over her body and her heart to Kazim.

The mental and intellectual worlds of these two individuals were as far apart as the sky and the earth are. Yet they felt as if their desires had found a refuge. In truth, they were drifting on an ocean of dark forces like aimless twigs of straw.

❦

A year went by. Kazim's marriage was settled. The ceremony soon approached. The bride was to arrive in four or five days. The house was overflowing with guests and there was a lot of work to be done. Dulari disappeared on one of those busy nights. People searched for her far and wide and even though the police was involved in the search, she could not be traced. Everybody was suspicious about one of the servants. They believed that he had not only helped Dulari to run away but had also helped her to go into hiding. That servant

Angarey

was thrown out. Eventually, Dulari was found to be with the man. But she categorically refused to come back home.

Three or four months later, an aged servant from Sheikh Nazim Ali's house spotted Dulari in that locality of the city where the prostitutes lived. The old man, who had known Dulari since her childhood, spent many hours persuading her to return until she finally agreed. The old man imagined that he would be rewarded and that the girl would be bailed out of trouble.

※

Dulari's return unsettled the whole house once again. She entered the house with her head bowed, covered with a white chadar. Anxiety was writ large on her face as she walked in and sat down on the floor in a corner. The maids were the first to arrive. They trickled in, stared at her from afar, expressed their regrets and walked away. Shortly, Nazim Ali-sahib entered the women's quarters—he had come to know that Dulari had returned. He came to where Dulari was sitting. He was a busy man and hardly participated in domestic matters. He barely had any time to deal with such minor issues? He raised his voice and, from a distance, said to Dulari, 'Stupid girl! Never do something so foolish again!' Having said this, he went out to work. After that, the choti sahibzaadi quietly came to Dulari, though she was careful not to come too close. There was nobody else around. She had grown up with Dulari and was deeply anguished about her running away from home. The modest, chaste and unpolluted

Dulari

Haseena-begum pitied the poor girl with all her heart but could not comprehend how any girl could abandon and step out of the safety of the home where she had spent her whole life. And what had come of it? She had had to sell her body and face poverty and humiliation! It was true that she was a londi, but did running away from home improve her lot in any way?

Dulari was sitting with her head bowed. Haseena-begum assumed that she was ashamed of what she had done. It was sheer ingratitude to run away from the home she had grown up in. But she had already been punished enough for that; even Khuda accepts the confessions made by sinners. While it was true that her reputation has been completely destroyed, it was not as significant a loss for a londi as it would have been for a respectable woman. She could be married off to one of the servants. Everything would be back to normal again, soon. She said in a tender voice, 'Dulari, what is this that you've done?' Dulari lifted up her head, looked at her childhood friend with eyes brimming with tears and then, once again, looked down.

Haseena-begum was walking away when Begum-sahiba herself appeared. She had a victorious smile on her face. She stood very close to Dulari who continued to sit quietly with her head bowed low. Begum-sahiba started, 'You shameless girl! So you have returned to where you had run away from, except that you have lost your honour now. The whole world is spitting at you, condemning you. This can be the only result of bad deeds ...' However, despite the harsh words,

Angarey

Begum-sahiba was actually glad that Dulari had returned. The chores of the household weren't being satisfactorily taken care of since the day Dulari had left.

Everybody in the house gathered around Dulari and Begum-sahiba to watch this spectacle of admonishment. The sight of an unchaste, insignificant creature being disgraced brought to them an exaggerated sense of their own superiority and merit. The vultures preying on the dead bodies of animals do not realize that the defenceless body into which they jab their foul beaks are, despite being dead, better than those like them who are alive.

All at once, Kazim emerged from a nearby room along with his beautiful bride. He did not look at Dulari. Anger shining on his face, he said to his mother in a stern voice, 'Ammi, for God's sake, leave the unfortunate girl alone. She has been punished enough. Can't you see her condition?'

The girl didn't possess the strength she needed to endure these words. Her memory recreated those nights when she and Kazim would meet secretly, and her ears had become accustomed to his words of love. Kazim's marriage was like a dagger stuck into her heart. It was this jab, this injury, this heartlessness, that had brought her to where she was. And now he, too, had started saying these things. This deep anguish transformed Dulari into a figure of feminine majesty. She got up and glared at the whole gathering with an expression which made them leave one by one until no one remained. But that was merely the last, desperate attempt of an injured bird to take flight. That night, she disappeared once again.

Heaven Assured!
~ Sajjad Zahir ~

Though it is true that Lucknow is decaying, it still continues to be a centre of Islamic learning. Even in these tumultuous days, many Arabic madrasas have kept the flame of guidance burning bright. People who carry within them the fervour of righteousness come here from every corner of Hindustan, receive religious knowledge, and devote themselves to the task of upholding the greatness of Islam. Unfortunately, the two sects who have built their madrasas in Lucknow consider each other to be sinners. But if we were view the tutors and the disciples of these two groups with a calm eye, without presuming them to be communal, we could glimpse the virtuous radiance that lights up their hearts and minds. The long kurtas and gowns of the clerics, their shoes and slippers, their dopalli caps and their shaved heads were such that even the most beautiful, celestial houris would gladly pick each strand of hair in their unsullied beards and caress it with their eyelids. All this is certainly the unmistakable evidence of their purity and abstinence. Moulvi Mohammad Daud-sahib, celebrated for his wisdom, had been teaching in a madrasa for many years. He offered his prayers with such heartfelt sincerity that during the auspicious month of Ramzan he lost all sense of time and hardly realized that he had recited the *Quran* and offered namaaz through the night. When he dozed off during his classes the following day, his disciples naturally assumed that he was in the grip of some spiritual fervour and quietly slipped away.

The propitious month of Ramzan is a gift from God for every Muslim, especially during the searingly hot months of May and June. It is quite obvious that higher the degree of the ordeal endured, the greater is the merit earned. During these days of intense heat, every creature of God is like a tiger raging away on the path which leads to Him. Their parched features and sunken eyes shriek, All of you unprincipled and unfortunate people, riddled with doubt, gaze upon us! Look at our faces and be ashamed of yourself. The merciful, flawless God has taken away your ability to think, but learn from us how people trembling in awe of His power express their complete submission to Him!

While it is true that all days and nights during the month of Ramzan are meant for the worship of God, yet worship on Shab-e-Kadr, the twenty-seventh night, is said to be especially rewarding, for it is on this night that the doors of the realm of God are left wide open for the sinners to confess and for upright Muslims to amass unlimited merit. The people who spend this auspicious night praying and reciting the *Quran* are considered to be especially fortunate. Moulvi Daud-sahib never allowed such beneficial occasions to slip by. Who knows the number of sins people commit every second? Many kinds of ideas, both good and bad, keep raising their heads. Moulvi Daud-sahib's response to people who asked him to practice moderation was that it is difficult to predict the consequences of one's sins, especially when goodness is assessed on the Day of Judgement. It is crucial, then, to stock up on as much merit as possible.

Moulvi Daud-sahib, also known as the Maulana, was about fifty years old and though short in height, was physically strong. His complexion was wheatish, he sported a triangular beard, and his white hair was peppered with black. The Maulana had been married off when he was about nineteen or twenty years old, but his first wife had passed away giving birth to their eighth child. He remarried two years later, when he was forty-nine, but his second wife pestered him endlessly. There was an age gap of about twenty years between them. He often tried to tell her that the reason why he had greyed prematurely was chronic phlegm, but she would offer other kinds of evidence right away, which the Maulana could not challenge, and he was thus left with no option but silence.

A year passed after the Maulana was married, and Shab-e-Kadr arrived. That day the Maulana rested for an hour or so after iftar. He then bathed and went back to the mosque where a large number of Muslims had gathered. These worthy sons of God, tahmets tied around their waists, leaped up to greet Maulana Daud-sahib. The Maulana's face was radiant and his walking stick—a witness to the authenticity of his principles—seemed to hold complete sway over the crowd. Once the namaaz of Esha, the namaaz of the night, was offered, the accumulation of merit continued unabated till about two in the morning. After that, the Maulana ate the sargi, the pre-dawn meal, and began his trip back home. He yawned uncontrollably. His stomach was stuffed with delicacies like sheermal, pulao and kheer, and he sought repose. He managed to somehow reach home but the battle between body and soul continued ceaselessly. A couple of hours of the Shab-e-Kadr still remained, and could have been well spent in worship, but his body craved rest and sleep. Ultimately, this experienced worshipper resolved to be led by spirituality and rubbed his eyes to bid farewell to sleep.

Darkness ruled over the whole house; the lantern had no flame. The Maulana rummaged around in vain for a matchbox to light the lantern. His wife slept on her bed in a corner of the courtyard. Apprehensive, the Maulana crept up to his wife and timidly shook her by the shoulder. Moulvi-sahib's young wife was in deep slumber on that star-spangled summer night which had cooled off as it approached the morn. When she finally woke, she turned and in a soft, half-asleep voice, asked, 'What is it?'

The Maulana was not accustomed to this silky tone. He gathered courage and managed a single word: 'Matchbox.' Though near waking, Moulvi-sahib's wife was very much in the grip of slumber. The shadows of the night and the glitter of the stars had spilled magic over her youth. She caught hold of the Maulana's hand and pulled it towards herself. Putting her arms around his neck, she nuzzled his face and, sighing deeply, said, 'Come, lie down next to me.'

The Maulana's heart, too, cut a caper for a moment but, the very next instant, he recalled the longings of Havva, Adam's first lapse, the passion of Julekha, and Yusuf's tattered clothes. His memory summoned a complete list of the transgressions of women and helped to rein him in. It could have been his age, the dread of God, or spirituality—whatever the reason, the Maulana hastily slipped out of his wife's embrace, stood up tall, and asked in a thin voice, 'Where is the matchbox?'

In an instant, the woman's slumber as well as her passion evaporated and transformed into corrosive sarcasm. She sat up on her bed and, deliberately soaking her words in poison, said, 'You tottering old man! You father of eight! You fraud of a namaazi! You have destroyed my slumber. Matchbox? Matchbox! It must be somewhere, on some sill or the other.'

Nothing is more painful for an aged husband than to have his young wife call him old. Maulana shuddered but decided to keep quiet. He lit a lantern, spread out the ja-namaaz on a divan, and started reciting the *Quran*. Maulana's drowsiness might have disappeared but within half an hour, the food digesting in his packed stomach started to drain the strength from his body and weigh his eyelids down. The verses from the *Quran*, the Surah-e-Rehman, and the Maulana's soothing recitation worked as a lullaby. The Maulana grunted a few times and then slumped over on to the ja-namaaz.

The Maulana was dead to the world at first but soon began to feel as though he was standing in a pitch-dark field, alone and abandoned, trembling with fear. Gradually, the darkness was dispelled by light and a voice close to him said, 'Bow your head down low! You are in the province of God.' The words had barely been uttered when the Maulana dropped down to the ground in devotion. A thundering voice—instilling fear—reverberated in the sky around the Maulana and then reached his ears, 'My faithful follower, I am pleased with you! All your life you have been so deeply absorbed in serving me that you have managed to keep yourself away from wisdom and imagination, the two most evil forces that engender cynicism and atheism. Rationality and human reasoning are the worst adversaries of conviction and faith. You have been able to grasp this mystery and have never allowed the glow of uprightness to be dimmed by the rust of intellect. Your reward is the eternal heaven where all your wishes will be fulfilled.' Having made this announcement, the voice fell silent.

For some time, the Maulana was so much in awe of God's eminence that he did not have the courage to raise his head. He waited for his pounding heart to slow down and, still lying down, looked out of the corners of his eyes. The scene that presented itself was utterly unexpected. The lonesome field had become a splendid drawing room. The walls of the room were made out of precious stones and were decorated with delicate floral designs. It seemed as if the glittering red, green, yellow, golden and silver flowers and fruits would drop down from the walls at any time. Bright light filtered in through the walls with a kind of radiance that soothed the eyes. The Maulana sat up and looked around.

Astonishing! Amazing! There were about sixty or seventy windows on the walls, each one of which was as tall as an adult human being. At each window stood a houri. Wherever he turned his eyes, the Maulana saw the houris smiling at him and alluring him with gestures, but the Maulana, awkward and uncomfortable, immediately lowered his eyes. The reason why the most diligent devotee of the world was embarrassed was because all the houris were stark naked. His eyes then fell on his own body and he discovered that he, too, was in the same state of being—divinely undressed. He looked around anxiously to see if anyone was sniggering at him but could see no one besides the houris. Even though the shame at being exposed had not completely vanished, the sarcasm and ridicule of the world—the most compelling reasons for his shame—seemed entirely non-existent in heaven. The Maulana's apprehensions decreased and youthful blood began to race through his body once more, a youthfulness which would never seep away.

The Maulana stroked his beard, smiled, and walked towards one of the windows. The houri stepped towards him and the Maulana scanned her from head to toe. She had an enchanting smile, her skin had the whiteness of the champa flower and her eyes bore the keenness of a dagger.

Angarey

The Maulana could not take his eyes off of this heavenly vision. But can any human heart ever be content with just one thing? The Maulana walked on to the next window and then on to the next, pausing in front of each, scrutinizing every ravishing houri, taking in all her details. Each time he smiled in appreciation before moving on. All this while, he continued to mutter the darood, the holy words, under his breath. He was charmed by the dark curly hair, the pink cheeks, the ruddy lips, the shapely legs, the slim fingers, the intoxicating eyes, the pointed breasts, the delicate waist, and the warm stomach of one or the other of these houris.

He was finally bowled over by the coquetry of one of the houris. He skipped quickly into her closet and tightly embraced the divine creature. Their lips were still to be sealed together when loud laughter broke out behind him. Just as a wave of anger washed over the Maulana at this most ill-timed laughter, his dream broke and his eyes opened. The sun had risen. The Maulana was lying on his stomach on the ja-namaaz, hugging the holy book to his chest. His wife was standing close by, laughing.

Insomnia
~ Sajjad Zahir ~

Dhad dhad dhad dhad tikh tikh chhat tikh tikh tikh chhat chhat chhat!

An age has passed since I embraced silence and darkness. Darkness. Darkness. The eyes open after a moment. The stark whiteness of the pillow. Darkness, though not pitch dark. My eyes close again. But it's not pitch dark! Screwed my eyes shut but light still filters in. Why does it not become pitch dark? Why not? Why not?

All those tall claims about being my friend! Each one of them says at the slightest available opportunity, Do come, Akbar-bhai, I have been dying to get a glimpse of you. Hee, hee, hee. Let's hear something new. Here, have a cigarette. But he does understand. He really can appreciate the shers. But that other one, the unadulterated buffoon, is a complete idiot. Arre! You are wearing a new achkan! How does it

Angarey

matter to you, or to anybody else, whether I wear a new achkan or not? Do you want to be the only one with a new achkan? Understanding shers is impossible for someone like you; you can hardly even read one. You really frustrate me. Such insolence! But his elder brother pretends to be my friend. What's the point of such friendships? The only bond between us are my homilies which provide him with a little entertainment. So am I a comedian gratis? Have fun, then … Ya Khuda, do what wish, just don't make one poor. One gets tired of bending over backwards to flatter people. And these people, just because they have a little more money in their pockets, they seem to be beyond everything. But I did tell him one day that I am neither your servant nor your slave. The way he glowered at me! All I wanted to do was to pull on his ears and slap him. That would have set the bugger right.

Tap tap khat tap tap khat tap tap khat tap tap t…

Who could that be at this time of the night? He's surely going to die for this. And if it starts raining, he'll be so much worse off. It rained when I was in Lucknow, it rained heavily during a public meeting. Amin-ud-daulah Park had become a pond. But people there refused to budge even an inch. And what is it—what exactly—that people are ready to risk their lives for? They wait for Mahatma Gandhi. He'll be here. Soon. There he comes. There. There. There. There he is on stage … Jai, jai, jai … silence.

I want to tell all of you to stop wearing foreign clothes. This mischievous government… The water, then, completely

Insomnia

drenched all heads and flowed down the legs like gutters. The heavens were pissing! Mischievous government, mischievous government—my foot! The mischievous, unfit government is scared shit of this Gandhi. Aha, ha! Unfit, shit—what rhyming, Akbar-sahib! Mashallah! You are a born poet. How about writing a nationalist poem? How far can these tales of the lover and the beloved be stretched? Nation and nationalism can both go to hell! What has the nation done for me that I should abandon the lover and the beloved to dance to their tunes? But what puzzles me is why everybody is out to flay me when I've caused no harm to anybody. My clothes are filthy, they stink, so let me be. He looked at my cap and remarked that it has oil stains. Why don't you buy a new one? Why should I buy a new cap? A new cap. A new cap? What is so special about a new cap? Will it be studded with stars?

>Angusht numa thi kaj kulahi jinki
>Ve jootiyan chatkhate firte hain aaj

>Those who once used to wear stylish caps
>Drag their feet around in slippers today

>Hum auj-e-taala-e-lal-o-guhar ko ...[1]

---

[1] Part of a couplet by Ghalib the gist of which is: the jewels have achieved a lofty status by virtue of being affixed on your cap.

Angarey

Wah! Wah, wah! How absurd. Our Hindustan is the jewel in George V's crown. The British have stolen it and have left everybody dumbstruck! The bird of gold has flown away and we are left behind, clutching a few feathers. What do you want now? To lose these as well? Hang on to these. Hang on. Bravo! Well done. Don't give up. You lose that and you lose your dignity. What? Dignity? Did you say dignity? What good is dignity? I've grown up on meagre scraps—dry roti, salt—but what style, what brawn I possess! And it gets better if one starves, much better. Then all that one has is dignity and, above that, is only God Almighty ... Khudavand Paak, Allah, Baari-ta-a-la, Rabb-ul-izzat, Parmeshwar, Parmatma—let there be innumerable names. Hurry, hurry, hurry up. What happened? Spiritual satisfaction? That's it? Is that enough for you? But hell has settled in my stomach. Prayers don't fill stomachs, they just create a vacuum. Hunger becomes even sharper.

Bhow-wow, bhoo, bhoo ...

If this barking begins now, it will go on through the night. And the mosquitoes make the night so much worse. God forbid! A net curtain is very useful in the heat. It liberates one from the mosquitoes. But what is the point of this liberation? This labouring through the day, this shrieking and screaming, running around from one place to another, dying of the heat. Amma used to say, Akbar, don't run around in the sun. Come, come and lie down next to me. Listen child, you will get a heatstroke, my baby. An aeon has passed since then. All that seems like a distant dream. And Moulvi-sahib's praise.

Insomnia

Look at Akbar, you dim-witted boys! What zest for knowledge he has. A dream. All that seems like a dream. Me running back home with my bag and wooden slate. Amma holding me close in her lap. What comfort! What reassurance! But I am not fated to have these things. Not many could have survived the hard times I've faced. Anyway, what's the point of thinking about all that? The charity hospital, the nurses, the hospital, everybody sulking, and Amma's condition so bad that it was painful for her to even move a limb. Her spittoon was full of blood. Like little chunks of flesh. And I writing letters to everybody. The same people who called themselves our relatives. Welcome, Akbar-bhai, welcome! I haven't met you in ages... The same people. And their parents, too. What would they have lost had they helped us one little bit? They waste their money on all kinds of senseless things but become so stingy when a relative is in need. And then, God help us, they do it as though it were a great favour upon us. One day, I was out for a while when this gentleman's mother came to visit Amma. She had been there for only a few minutes when I reached. The fear of contracting infection was clearly visible on her face. Still, she had considered it her duty to call on the patient. A virtuous act! Then she started scolding me, Where did you go? Your mother is in no condition to be left alone. Such talk in front of the patient! I was mad with rage but I could do nothing. I was dependent on these people for the hospital expenses. My wife and children, too, were dependent on them... Anybody who had as much as even heard that I should be married had opposed the plan. But it was Amma's life's desire to see me married. I must get home Akbar's bride. That's my only wish in life now. People used to say, You don't have enough to eat. How can you get him married like this? Amma used to say it is God who gives us food. He is the one who supports us. When my marriage was settled and the date of the ceremony fixed, the same people who were opposed to it turned up. Whatever little Amma had saved up was spent on hospitality and in buying things. Gas lights, silk achkans, pulao, a music band, bolsters, fun, crowd. The food ran short. The cook stole. Badshah Ali-sahib's shoes were stolen, too. All hell broke loose. You buffoon, why did you not take care of your shoes? Ji huzoor, I am not at fault. There was a squabble about the meher, and then the discussion about the mowajjal and muajjal payments. The ritual unveiling of the bride's face and the ritual of paying respects to the elders. The teasing, the joking, the flowers, the abuses. The marriage was solemnized. Amma's wish was fulfilled... Muharram Ali, poor thing, is forty and still unmarried. Akbar-mian, do get me married. The devil really torments me at nights. Marriage! Delight! At least a well-wisher with whom one can talk to one's heart's content in privacy. A woman to love, to chat with and laugh with, to embrace, to love. Arre! Say yes, my dear, my life! My love! All that is precious in my life. My words are meaningless. My limbs, my whole body, every pore of my body... Why? Are you upset with me today? Arre! You have started weeping. For God's sake tell me. What is the matter? Just look at me. At least look at me. Why waste this short life in weeping? Uff, not like that! Like this. And, and come embrace me tight...

Insomnia

I am well acquainted with the nautch girls of Lucknow. I am not so destitute that I must gaze at the girls from a distance, sigh, and do nothing? Welcome huzoor! Akbar-sahib, is it fair that you should ignore us for so long? Do oblige us with one of your beautiful new ghazals. Should I sing it? Here, do oblige us and accept this paan. Oh! Just relax. Relax for a while. Do please excuse me today—another time. I am always at your service... Slaves to money. Does she think that I am penniless? She saw the money and immediately agreed. What should I sing for you, huzoor? The beat of the tabla, the lilt of the sarangi, the singing, the playing. And then there I was, there she was, the entire night. Only a kafir would have fallen asleep. Those wakeful nights, the headaches the next day, the exhaustion, the mental tension. When Amma was ill, I used to sit for hours next to her bed, almost stuck to it. And her cough ... it scared even me at times. Each time she coughed, it seemed as if her chest was receiving a fresh wound; as if each breath was a sharp blade slicing through lesions. And that rattle in her chest—like a hot summer wind blowing through old ruins. Scary... My mother began to scare me. She wasn't really my mother, that hollow shape of bones and skin? I used to put my hand on hers and press it lightly. Her half-open, half-shut eyes would turn towards me. Her eyes would be on me. Only those eyes in that frail, feeble, lifeless body of hers were alive. Her lips would tremble. Amma. Amma. What is it you want to say? Ji! I would take my ear close to her lips. She would lift her hand and place it on my head. It was as if her fingers had somehow entangled themselves in my hair and she had no desire to extricate them. It's late. Go. Go and get some sleep. Amma lies on the bed like this. One month, two months, three months, one year, two years, a hundred years, a thousand years. God's messenger of death turned up. Impertinent. Uncivilized. Get lost! Go! Go away or I'll chop your tail off. And then you'll be reprimanded by the big boss. Are you grinning? Why are you still standing here, teeth bared? You messenger! I'll put you in your place. You ... messenger... your...

Who cares for this paltry world; and you too, mian Akbar! The whole world has to be shown its proper place, Akbar-mian. You, too. Just look at yourself. A strong breath can blow you away. And what a great poet he imagines himself to be! A little occasional praise in the soiree and he thinks... Actually, he can hardly afford to think. Poor thing! He can only think if his dear wife will allow him a little space. But all she does is complain. Weep and whine. Our clothes are in tatters; the children have lost their caps; buy him a new one... As if my own cap is new. Where did it get lost? How would I know where it got lost? I can't run after him all the time. I have enough work to do. Washing, stitching, running the house—everything is solely my responsibility. I don't have time to display my skill at shers like some others do. Just get one thing straight. I have a lot of work to do. I'd invited this. I put my hand into the beehive and it is difficult to save myself from being stung. What a razor-sharp tongue! Mashallah, chashm-e-baddoor, may God save you. You know only too well that I don't have proper clothes. Your son walks about

Insomnia

naked but you behave as if you have nothing to do with all of this. As if they are somebody else's children. Hai Allah! It's my misfortune... Now the weeping will begin. Mian Akbar, it's in your best interest to quietly slip away. There's no need to be embarrassed. Your valour, your manliness, won't be diminished at all. Aye Khuda! Why did you create woman? It is not possible for a feeble, pathetic man like me to handle this liability, to keep her in custody. And I know very well what exactly will happen on the Day of Judgement. These women will shriek and screech. They will put on such enticing airs and wink so that even Allah-mian will scratch his beard, wondering how to deal with them. What will this Day of Judgement be like? The sun hanging really low. The scorching heat of May and June would not even compare. The suffering. Tauba tauba! Arre tauba! These mosquitoes are driving one to distraction. Sleep is out of question. Pinn, pinn, chhat—one dead! Why do these annoying, lawless creatures buzz into the ears? I hope Khuda will resolve to have no mosquitoes around on the Day of Judgement. But who knows? Nothing is certain. After all, what was the rationale for creating mosquitoes and bedbugs? Who knows whether the mosquitoes and bedbugs nibble at the messengers of God, too! Nothing is certain. Nothing is certain. What is your name? What is mine? Nothing is certain. Wah wa... wah! Only God knows what we don't. God! God and bawd and pod! Wrong! Its people not pod. Mian Akbar, don't cross your limits. What else is it?

Angarey

Bahr-e-rajaz mein daal ke bahre ramal chale.[2] Khoob! Woh tifl kya karega jo ghutne ke bal chale. Brilliant! What do you expect from a child who crawls on all fours?

Sour grapes! Do you enjoy the tarty flavour? Enjoy? How does it matter what we enjoy? One must also get one's hands on it. I enjoy riding in the horse-carriage but the moment I approach it, the horse kicks me so hard that I must run away as fast as my legs can carry me. And what else do I enjoy? My love. You are my life. Just that I love you more than my life... Forget it. I know what all your sweet talk is worth... Why? What happened? What happened? I can't tolerate this humiliation. You know I labour through the day like a londi. Actually, worse than a londi. Since the day I have been married into this house, I haven't seen any servant stick around for even a month. In more than a year I have had no respite whatsoever. Akbar's wife, do this. Akbar's wife, do that. Arre! Arre! What happened? You've started weeping again. I beg of you. Take me away from here. Take me somewhere else. I am a decent person, from a respectable family. I've been through a lot, tolerated enough, but I can't put up with being abused. Abuse. Abuse? What abuse? Has it come to this now? My wife being abused? Allah! Ya Allah! That wicked begum's neck in my hands. Her eyes pop. Her tongue hangs out. The world cleansed of evil... Leave me, for God's sake. It was my

---

[2]The quoted line is by the poet Insha-allah-khan-insha. He is commenting on poets who start with one metre and slip into another inadvertently.

Insomnia

mistake. Forgive me, Akbar. I've done some good to you in the past... Of course you've been kind to me. I'm deeply obliged to you for that. But now your end is near. What made you think that you could abuse my wife? That's it. It is all over for you now. Make your last wish. Actually, chopping your head off will be better than wringing your neck. The head dangles free, held merely by hair! The tongue hangs loose to one side. Blood drips. The eyes stare. Ya Allah! What has happened to me? A sea of blood. I am drowning in a sea of blood. Red clots are hurtling at me from all sides. Here it comes! Here comes another one! Now they will explode on my head... Can this be hell? But these are clots, not balls of fire. I am on fire! Every follicle of hair on my body is on fire. Run! Oh, run! Help me. I am being reduced to ashes. My hair is singed. Water! Water! Can nobody hear my cries? For God's sake, pour water on my head. What? Will I have to walk bare feet on these glowing embers? What? Will my eyes be pierced with red-hot skewers? What? Will I get only boiling water to drink? What, what, what? Will I be made to swallow pus? Why are these flames approaching me? Will these flames burn me or these pointed spokes blind me? The pain of the wound and of the burn. Whose scream is this? I have heard this voice before. Uoo, uoo, uoo ... uoo, uoo, uo, uo, uo, u... it is moving away. What is my son's offence? Which crime is he being punished for? My son is only four years old. He should be pardoned. *I*'m the criminal. *I*'m the guilty one. Who approaches? Arre! God save me! She has snakes entwined around her neck. They're nuzzling at her

Angarey

breasts. Huzoor, aadab arz hai! Huzoor! Have you forgotten me? This helpless, ill-fated one? I am Munni-jaan. Some thumri? Some dadra? A ghazal? Aye, hai! You look scared, huzoor. These snakes will not harm you. There's a funny story about them too. When I had just entered this place, the Daroga-sahib had said to me, bi Munni jaan! The sarkar has ordered that five scorpions be presented to you for your service. I began to tremble, huzoor. I have detested scorpions since I was a child. I pleaded, huzoor, but Daroga-sahib said that it was his duty to execute the order passed by the government. Then I told him to take me to the durbar so that I could appeal to them about this. Daroga-sahib was a good man. He made me sit close, stroked my cheeks and finally agreed. First, I had to wait for several hours. Daroga-sahib informed me that the government was in council with some holy men. I would receive a hearing only after they finished. When I heard this, I tried to peep in. But the sentry at the door, the bully, pushed me away. Anyway, huzoor, I was finally called in. My heart was palpitating. I was nervous about what would happen in there. I fell on my knees as soon as I entered the durbar of the government. It seemed as if I'd lost my voice. Daroga-sahib reported my matter. I was then ordered to stand up. I, huzoor, stood up. And then sarkar, the boss himself, came close to me. He had a full, white beard and flawless complexion. He looked at me and smiled. He then took me by my hand and entered the room nearby. Huzoor, I was completely bewildered ... but, huzoor, he had aged only as far as his looks were concerned. I have not seen

Insomnia

such a masculine and virile man in the whole world. And with your grace, huzoor, many a noblemen have visited me in my time. Anyway, huzoor, sarkar then announced that my punishment cannot be waived because his justice is meted out equally to all. But, instead of the scorpions, I was given these two snakes which keep licking at my breasts. Actually, huzoor, the truth is that this gives me no grief. In fact, I like it... But you are scared of me, Akbar-sahib! Aye huzoor Akbar-sahib, some thumri, some dadra, a ghazal...

Ya Allah! The merciful one! Save me from the fires of hell! I, an insignificant sinner, stand here in front of you praying for forgiveness. But I cannot bear to be humiliated. My wife is being abused, but what can I do? Should I starve myself? A skull on top of a skeleton walking—khat, khat, tap, tap—on the road. Akbar-sahib, where did all your flesh disappear? Where is your skin? Yes, sir. I am dying of hunger. I have fed my flesh to the vultures. I had a tabla fashioned from my skin and gifted it to bi Munni jaan. What an amazing idea! Don't you agree? If you are envious of me, then Bismillah, embark on this path yourself. Just follow me, extol me and do it. I recommend no one, commend no one. I am free like the breeze. A breeze of emancipation is blowing these days. You may be famished, your stomach may be crying out for food but you are ensnared by freedom. Death or freedom. I fancy neither death nor freedom. Somebody sate my hunger. Fill my empty stomach.

Pinn, pin, pin ... chhat, what the hell! These mosquitoes... Tann, tann, tann ... tann, tann.

The Same Uproar, Once Again
~ Sajjad Zahir ~

'Religion is a remarkable thing. In grief, in trouble, during letdowns, at times when we are bewildered and at our wits' end; when, like an injured beast, we look all around with defenceless, fearful eyes, which power is it that sustains our sinking hearts? Of course, it is religion! And religion is rooted in faith—fear and faith. Religion cannot be described in words. We cannot comprehend it thus. It is an internal state …'

'What? An internal state?'

'This is no joke. Religion is a heavenly glow and it is in the radiance of this glow that we gaze upon the spectacle of creation. It is an internal…'

'For God's sake, talk about something else. You have absolutely no idea what my internal state is like right now. I have a severe stomach ache and I certainly have no need

The Same Uproar, Once Again

for any heavenly glow at the moment. What I need is a laxative ... '

I was immersed in a novel one night when somebody padded silently into my room. I looked up to find mian Iblees—the Devil himself—standing before me.

'Mian Iblees,' I asked, 'why do you visit me at this hour? I'm busy with this truly gripping novel. And, once again, you want me to close my book and get into a pointless discussion about religion with you. I think it better to read a book than to stress my mind with religious matters. You will not succeed in sowing the seed of doubt in my heart.'

Just as I uttered these words, Iblees turned around and started to walk out of the room. I had begun to feel guilty for having ill-treated a messenger of God when he turned back towards me and said in a voice heavy with grief, 'I'm not Iblees, I'm Jibraeel. I brought messages from Khuda to Hazrat Mohammad Saheb. I don't want to blame you for mistaking me for Iblees. He too, after all, is a messenger of God like me. It's not just you, people with much better judgement have mistaken me for Iblees and have thrown me out of their homes. Even some apostles have committed this blunder. In truth, I am the messenger of goodness. My countenance exudes purity. Perhaps people would have treated me differently if I had been as good-looking as Iblees. And, by the way, how did you come to the conclusion that I wanted to discuss religion with you? What have I to do with discussion or debate? Every debate, since it is founded on intellect and logic, is an evil thing. Religion is rooted in faith. If your faith is deep-seated, then God himself will support you in religious discussions. And if you have God's support on your side, why do you need intellect? Religion is truly excellent ...'

※

Intellect and integrity, the skies and the earth, human beings and divine messengers, God and the devil—what am I thinking about? It is the rain which quenches the parched earth and spreads the fragrance of fulfilment all around. People die of starvation in famines. It seems as if the bones and ribs of old men, children, young men and women, with sunken eyes and pale faces, are just about to rip through their wrinkled skin. The ache of hunger; cholera, vomiting, loose motions, flies, death! There's nobody to bury or cremate the dead. The bodies rot and give off a nauseating stench.

※

A rich man had a pet dog named Shera. The dog usually stayed within the compound of his master's house and was fed at regular intervals. Of course, he occasionally attacked the street dogs. This habit became more compulsive as he grew older. When the scrawny street dogs of the neighbourhood would see Shera approach, they would abandon their bitches, scamper off to a safe distance, and bark at him from there. Shera, busy with the bitches, would not even glance at the

The Same Uproar, Once Again

street dogs. Incidentally, a dog twice the size of Shera arrived in the neighbourhood and made up his mind to confront him. The two dogs fought a couple of times. During these fights, the bitches would run away and all the street dogs, and their leader, would get together and attack Shera. Gradually, it so happened that not only could Shera not step out of his compound, but the gang of street dogs would even enter Shera's courtyard to attack him. Whenever this happened, the dogs would make such a racket that it was impossible to hear anything else. If the servants of the house happened to be around, they would rush to save Shera, and would manage to do so, but with great difficulty. Shera was wounded several times, after which he took to hiding inside the house. The street dogs had achieved complete victory.

One day, Shera was strolling in the courtyard of his house when, under the leadership of the big dog, the band of stray dogs attacked him once more. People inside the house were asleep at the time, but the commotion jolted everybody out of sleep. The rich man, Shera's master, also rushed out. When he saw what was happening, he went back into the house and came back out carrying a gun. He shot the big dog dead and the others ran away. The wounded Shera began wallowing at his master's feet. The vile, wretched street dogs had been crushed. The well-trained, purebred dog, imported from overseas, was finally rescued and began, once again, to have a good time.

Angarey

What is humanity?

The river Gomati has been flowing for thousands of years. It floods, wipes out the settlements on its banks, and then carries on flowing gently, like it always has. There is a tiny temple on the river bank. It seems that its foundations were laid on sand which was washed away by the river. The temple leans to one side but still manages to stand. It is, however, certain that the temple will soon vanish. Its ruins will stay for a while and then the river will begin to flow over the spot where the temple once stood.

Today is a festival—the day of the holy bath. A crowd has collected around the ghats and the temples on the river bank. People are chanting mantras and taking holy dips in the river. The water in the river looks dirty. Rose and marigold petals are being tossed up and down by the water. Clusters of flowers, leaves, small pieces of wood, cigarette stubs, bits of shiny adornments that have fallen off from women's clothes, dead fish and other debris lie piled up at some spots near the shore.

The Gomati river, the dog Shera, the dead fish, the clouds floating in the skies, and the rotting corpses—everything is protected by the grace of God.

༄

The young son of the sweeper Kallu has been bitten by a snake. It is the rainy season and he had been sleeping in the courtyard. Near dawn, a snake bit him on his left elbow.

The Same Uproar, Once Again

He got up at about five in the morning, spotted the mark on his arm, and felt a little sore. He showed the mark to his mother and, thinking it to be the bite of some ordinary insect, got busy with sweeping. Kallu the sweeper, his wife and his children all work for the same family. He receives a salary of fifteen rupees a month and a small room in the servant quarters in which Kallu, his wife, his two daughters and his son stay. The sahib who gives Kallu fifteen rupees a month, one small room, the occasional leftovers and old, worn-out clothes is no less than God for him.

Kallu's son could not work for more than ten or fifteen minutes. His head began to reel and he felt a tremor course through his body. By about six o' clock, he was in bed, writhing in pain. His mouth began to foam and his eyes turned stony. The poison had entered every nerve in his body and death finally clasped him in its merciless grip. His parents began to weep. The information that Kallu's son had been bitten by a snake spread through the household. People suggested some or the other treatment.

Kallu's master's son was charitable and kind-hearted. He came to Kallu's tiny room, touched his son, and gave him medicines with his own hands. But Kallu's dingy, dark room was so filthy and smelt so bad that the master's son could not stay for even five minutes. After all, there is a limit to being charitable and kind-hearted. He went back home, had a good bath, changed his clothes and put a perfumed handkerchief to his nose. Only then did he begin to feel better. As far as Kallu's son is concerned, the poor thing died at about one o'clock. The sound of crying and howling from the room went on till late in the night and threw a pall of sorrow over the whole house. Kallu took an advance of ten rupees to perform the last rites. The dead body of Kallu's son was taken away at about nine or ten at night.

Hamid-sahib has been crazy about Sultana, a cousin distantly related to him. Hamid-sahib has seen Sultana-begum only from a distance and has never exchanged more than a few words with her. But what need does the blaze of love have for words, conversation and familiarity? Hamid-sahib smouldered within himself, swayed as he read out shers, and sometimes even penned down a ghazal under the influence of love. At nights, he would sit quietly near the river, sighing deeply. His two close friends were the only ones who knew about his obsession. They commended Hamid for keeping his love a secret. That was exactly the way in which respectable people should conduct themselves:

> Dekhna bhi to unhe door se dekha karna
> Sheva-e-ishq nahi husn ko ruswa karna

> Gaze upon your love, but from afar
> For disgracing the beloved is not the custom of love

Hamid probably did not go to his uncle's house more

than once a week. There was, however, no limit to his restlessness throughout the day before the visit. The poet quite rightly says:

Vada-e-vasl chu savad nazdeek
Aatish-e-shauk tez targaradda

As the moment of meeting approaches
The flame of desire glows keen

When Hamid's friends saw the state he was in, they said:

Ishq par zor nahin, hai ye woh aatish Ghalib
Ki lagaye na lage aur bujhaye na bane

Love, says Ghalib, follows no instruction
Its flame can neither be quenched nor lit on command

Hamid-sahib either smiled coyly; became upset and anxious; or, placing his hand on his heart, pleaded with his friends not to tease him.

Sultana-begum was, of course, very respectable. It was not proper that words like love and beloved be as much as uttered by women of respectable homes. She had probably never looked Hamid-bhai in the eye and talked to him but, when she saw Hamid-bhai nervous and awkward in front of her, she wondered if this was what was known as love. Hamid-bhai's love was completely chaste and thus, if it

Angarey

ever so happened that he was alone in a room with Sultana begum for a few minutes, all he did was to sigh deeply. He did not express his love through any other 'illegitimate' means. It was in this manner that the story of love carried on for a long time.

After Hamid-sahib found a job, he started thinking about marriage. His parents were also equally concerned about the matter. Sultana-begum's mother, too, was on the lookout for a groom for her daughter and it was with great difficulty that Hamid-sahib was finally able to convey to his mother his great desire to marry Sultana begum.

The communiqué for the proposed marriage, the payaam, was conveyed but Sultana-begum's mother hated the very sight of Hamid-mian's mother. Severe hostilities had always existed between the two ladies. Even when Hamid-mian's mother was dressed in the best clothes and jewellery, Sultana-begum's mother found some reason or the other to criticize and ridicule her. If one of them happened to wear a piece of jewellery that the other didn't possess, it was quite certain that at the next meeting, the other would be found wearing a similar or even a better piece. Any maid thrown out of one house was certain to find employment in the other.

Sultana-begum's mother merely smiled and evaded any clear response to the payaam that had arrived from Hamid-mian's house. She was on the lookout for a suitable match for Sultana-begum and planned to openly reject Hamid-mian's proposal once she had fixed a match. Hamid-mian's mother, well versed with schemes of this kind, was angered

The Same Uproar, Once Again

beyond measure. When a suitable, accomplished and well-employed boy was available within the family, then what was the point of getting Sultana married to someone outside? But Hamid-mian's love was genuine. He asked his mother to keep trying and a long time elapsed. It was God's will that Sultana-begum's mother found no other suitable groom for her.

Sultana begum turned nineteen. Her mother could not wait any longer and finally agreed. Hamid-mian got married to Sultana-begum. A little more than two years have passed since the marriage. The lover's wish was fulfilled. With God's grace, they have two children, too.

※

The night is cold. A poor woman lying on a loose-stringed charpoy in a small, dark room is groaning in pain. Her agony is so intense that drawing each breath is torture for her. The woman is to deliver a baby.

※

A poor woman, hiding from everybody under the cover of night, went out to meet her penniless lover. She met this man whenever she could.

The pleasure of love, the anguish of death! Why are these mountains, their lofty peaks knocking the skies, still standing firm? The waves in the ocean, the ticking of the clock, the sound of water dripping drop by drop, silence—and the heartbeat. A moment of love! The sound of blood racing through blood vessels. The eyes carry on a conversation. They listen. You pig, you villain, you idiot, you bastard—abuses and the harsh, fiery heat of the sun. It seems like it will scorch the skin and melt the bones.

※

A landlord and his farmhand who does not have enough money to pay the land tax. The son has sent a second letter to his father, demanding more money. He must pay the fees for his law course in the next four days. The father extracts money from peasants to educate his son.

※

The snakes are slithering all around. Black long snakes that dance with their hoods raised. Who should kill them? And how?

The thunder of the monsoon clouds! And from within the silence of the mountains gushes the roar of a waterfall. The fields, lush with swaying green plants; the deafening crack of a gun. Then, the agonized wail of a wounded crane—kaanye! kaanye! kaanye!

A Trip to Delhi
~ Rashid Jahan ~

'My sweet sister, do let me come in, too,' said a voice from the verandah and, along with it, entered a girl wiping her hands with the edge of her kurta.

Mallika-begum was the first amongst her friends to travel in a train, even though the journey was only from Faridabad to Delhi. The women from the mohalla had gathered around to listen to the accounts of her travel.

'Come if you want! As far as I am concerned, I am tired of repeating the same story ever so often. Only God knows how many times I have told it. I boarded a train here and reached Dilli. And there, one of his—I mean, my husband's—associates, a station master, met him. And then my dear husband left me along with the luggage and disappeared. And I, wrapped in a burqa, was left sitting atop the luggage. On the one hand this burqa troubled me and, on the other, the

Angarey

wanton men milling around! Men, as you know of course, are dissolute to begin with and, if they see a single woman sitting alone like I was, they just keep hovering around. Just imagine, I didn't even have a chance to chew a paan. Some of these men coughed, others mumbled, some others passed comments. I almost died of dread! Only God knows how hungry I was. And bua, what do you know? Delhi station is much, much bigger than any fort that you can think of. One can keep looking far into the distance and all one sees is the station and only the station, stretched out endlessly. Train tracks, engines, goods trains all around! And what terrified me most were those blackened men who live in the engine.'

'Who are these people who live in the engine?' somebody interrupted.

'Those who live there? Well ... I really don't know, bua. These were men in blue uniforms—some bearded and some clean-shaven. They can hold on to moving engines with one hand and hang out of them. Just a mere glimpse of them sends tremors through the heart. And there are so many sahibs and memsahibs on the Delhi station! It is just impossible to count them. They hold hands and walk about, talking in some gibberish. Indians keep staring at them with unblinking eyes. The scoundrels deserve to be blinded! One of them started saying to me, "Come on, do let me sneak a quick look! Just a tiny peep at your face!" I immediately ...'

Somebody teased, 'So, did you not allow it?'

'May Allah be always with me, bua! Did I go there to show my face to these ruffians? My heart skipped a beat

A Trip to Delhi

...' and then, changing her countenance, she added, 'don't interrupt me if you wish to listen.'

Complete silence fell over the assembly. Such spicy narrations rarely happened in Faridabad and women travelled long distances to listen to Mallika's story.

'Yes bua, the hawkers there are very different from the ones we have here. Many of them wear clean khaki clothes. Some wear white but many others also wear dhotis that are grimy and unwashed. A lot of them carry baskets and others run around pushing closed carts with paan, bidi, cigarettes, dahi-vadas, toys and sweets. A cart stopped next to me. The commotion that followed could have ruptured your eardrums!

'On the one hand, the coolies keep screaming and, on the other, the vendors go on with their non-stop chatter. It is enough to make one deaf! The passengers almost climb on top of each other, and amidst all this was I—poor woman—sitting atop the luggage. I must have been kicked and pushed around by thousands of people. I kept praying to God under my breath to save me, "Jalto jalal to, aai balaa ko taal tu!" Finally, after all the hitches, after all the prayers, the train started to move and then began the scuffles between the passengers and the coolies.

'"I'll charge one rupee!"

'"No, I'll give you two annas!"

'This must have gone on for at least an hour. It was only after all this was settled that the station was finally cleared out. Of course, it had still not been completely emptied.

Angarey

The hoodlums on the station were still around.

'After about two hours, I spotted him—my husband—twirling his moustaches. He asked me ever so casually, "Should I get some pooris or something else if you are hungry? Will you eat? I have already eaten at a hotel."

'I said, "For God's sake, take me home. I've had enough of this outing, enough! I know now that I should refuse even a visit to heaven with you. Oh, what a great trip you've brought me on!'

'The train to Faridabad was ready to leave. He ushered me in and then sat down next me, sulking. "Your wish!" he said, "it is entirely your wish if you don't want to enjoy your trip to Delhi."'

Masculinity

~ Mahmuduzzafar ~

Look, my wife is leaving. The smile which people said once brought peace and contentment to me has vanished from her lips. A mere skeleton is left behind. Her harrowing appearance is evidence of chronic disease. The fear of death is clear on her face. Instead of intimacy and love, her eyes reflect estrangement, a hatred for me. Actually, that is just what I deserve. The cause of this hatred is that unborn child, whose head she still thinks is stuck in her pelvis, sucking her life away. Who could have imagined that my wife would end up hating me on her deathbed? There is nothing that I have not done to save her from suffering and death. But wait. I have, in fact, ended up becoming the cause of her death. I am the one who brought pain and agony to her. There can be no limit to men's ignorance and idiocy. But it will also not be correct to say that I fell prey to ignorance

Angarey

and idiocy. I confess that I was a prisoner of my own ego.

We were married at an age when we could not have been expected to have the ability to appreciate each other's emotions. But I do not want to put the responsibility of the mishap, which occurred later, at either destiny's doorstep or blame events which I could not have controlled.

I never really fell in love with my wife. And how could I? The tracks of our lives did not intersect. My wife lived in the narrow and dark lanes of tradition while I walked the broad and well-lit roads of the new age. Still, there were times when I went to other countries and was separated from her for long years, that my heart became restive for her. She, of course, continued to live in her ancient, impregnable fort and in the moments when I felt surfeited by the fruitless, flirtatious encounters of my life, I often dreamt of the chaste and loyal woman who was ready to sacrifice everything for me without seeking anything in return. Whenever I felt this, I had an irresistible desire to meet her. I was once in the grip of such an emotion when I received a letter from her. I became restless and immediately started my journey home, a distance of six thousand miles. She had written:

> I have just taken out your letter from under my pillow and read it all over again. It is really short. You were probably busy with your work when you wrote it. Anyway, I have no complaints about that. I just want to be informed about your well-being. It is enough for me that you are happy and well. Since I have fallen ill,

Masculinity

I do nothing besides thinking of you. I wonder about all the unfamiliar things you do there and all the new people you meet. I cannot walk and so all I do is to lie on the bed and let my imagination run wild. I sometimes get immense pleasure from this and at other times it brings me deep agony. I feel deeply upset when people enquire about my health and offer all kinds of unsolicited advice. These people, of course, have no idea of the ailment that plagues me. Actually it is for their own satisfaction that they show me pity. I have become a burden even for my parents. They must surely be wondering how I continue to be a liability to them even after they had got me married. The consequence of all this is that I always try to conceal my despair and pain. And my parents always try to impress upon me how deeply they are concerned about my illness. In short, there exists nothing but pretension on both sides. I don't want to complain to you about anything and neither have I ever wanted you to be distracted from your work. The mere fact that you have not forgotten me and that you occasionally write to me is enough. Actually, sometimes I feel that it is better that you stay away from me. I dread to think that I may lose you, that I may become a stranger for you in the way in which I have become for everybody else after my illness. I am scared that you too might go away from me after seeing my chronically poor condition. Being where you are, so far away, you can only imagine how poor my health is; as much as I imagine you being my closest friend and confidant—something that my heart yearns for.

A wave of love and passion washed over me when I read this letter. I felt that it was my duty to go to her, and embrace her, even though she was in the grip of disease. I wanted to establish that nothing could possibly intrude into the sphere of my love. I wanted to let her know that I was, in truth, the close confidant that she desired. I concluded that I was as guilty and culpable as she was unsullied and blameless. I was weighed down by the notion that I was obliged to treat her with love. And thus I started for home.

I had still not finished my journey when my feelings began to change. That initial pristine emotion vanished and my mind started asking minor, routine questions. What would be my means of livelihood now? Who would I continue to befriend from amongst my friends? In what manner would I meet my in-laws; should I talk to them properly or ignore them? And so on. The earlier, intense craving to meet my wife was waning. The recollection of the tedium of daily life knocked out my desires and my enthusiasm. After I arrived home, the problems I had anticipated confronted me as unavoidable, ugly realities in flesh and blood. The old, nostalgic world that I had conjured up in my mind existed nowhere in reality. Quite contrary to my imagination, I found myself in a world that was narrow, orthodox, dark, illiterate and cruel. Most of the people who came to receive me at the station were vulgar, deceitful, ignorant, worthless

Masculinity

ruffians. They welcomed me with great joy. I was garlanded and was the subject of much conversation. The same old unsophisticated jokes were cracked and scores of people were foul-mouthed. Celebrations and feasting continued for many days. It was only after everything had ended that I was released from their company. During all this time I could meet my wife only for short spans of time even though her greasy, oily hair, her weak body and her pale visage continued to haunt me through all the feasting and celebrations.

After all visitors had left, I finally went to my wife and sat next to her on the bed. She continued to lie motionless and did not look at me at all. For a while I watched the movement of her breasts as they rose and fell with every breath. I then took her shrivelled hand in mine. We just sat like that for a while. I then said, 'See! I am here with you now. Say something. Why are you so quiet?'

She answered, 'What can I say? Of course, you are here.'

It dawned on me, all at once, that this was not going to work. I, however, recalled what I had resolved and said rather quickly, 'Wah! You do have to say a lot to me. Tell me how you were and what all you did when I was not here. Tell me everything. After all, you have not talked to me for such a long time. Now you must compensate me for all that. Do you remember that you had once written to me, saying that you desire a close friend and confidant? I am that person and I have come to you only so that I stay close to you at all times.' I, however, felt that all my efforts were in vain. It was apparent from my words that, much like rote learning,

Angarey

they were superficial, lacked all spontaneity, and brought little consolation to my wife. For a few moments I still lived with the hope that she had been successfully deceived by my insincerity. But that was only till she restlessly took hold of my cap and began pulling at it in agitation. What she then said convinced me of my abject failure.

'What can I say? For me there is no difference between day and night, but why are you so quiet? You must have had many new experiences, you must have dealt with many important matters. Talk about all those things to me. The strange things there, all kinds of machines, different kinds of people, a new life! You often wrote to tell me how you were not able to find spare time to write to me about all these things, but, now, you are here with me. At least now you have the time.'

She had deliberately attacked my self-centeredness. I now realized that the years of physical distance between us had failed to effect even a minor change in our relationship. We still remained strangers, we still stood on the two separate banks of a river. And, above all, we had again begun to deceive each other.

I said, 'Yes, of course. I have many things to tell you. We must decide what we would like to do together. But, for that to happen, you must regain your health quickly. We will speak about all this once you begin to feel better again. Till that happens, you must rest quietly, in peace. Do not stress you heart and mind. You have perhaps exhausted yourself because of my arrival. You must rest and not be anxious. All

Masculinity

right? I will leave, now, and you must go to sleep.'

I let her hand fall, got up, and left.

After that, I did not try to interact with her and neither did I discuss anything very specific with her for long. I would visit her once or twice a day, merely to inquire about her health and, after saying a few casual things, I would come away and immerse myself in work. Coincidentally, my own work was not proceeding too well during those days and I had a lot of free time. Gradually, I veered towards my old friends and began to spend a great deal of time with them. In the process, I cultivated many of their worthless habits as well as their vices. I started playing cards, drinking alcohol and indulging in meaningless banter all over again. I used to consider myself a connoisseur of music and soon ended up being a patron of the well-known nautch girls of the city. Under these circumstances, it was entirely understandable for me to have a mistress, too. These were the different ways in which we decided to spend our aimless and meaningless lives. Those among us who had travelled abroad spiced up all this by telling tall tales about our masculine profligacy to impress others.

Nevertheless, it was impossible for me to get rid of my wife. Due to her bad health, I was continuously pestered by a string of letters from friends and relatives which incessantly troubled me with enquiries about her well-being. Some offered advice, while others criticized me; some sympathized a little and still others much too excessively. My life had become hell because of all this. My liberated lifestyle

Angarey

constantly needled my in-laws. Their real fear was that I might abandon their daughter completely. To add to my troubles, my mother began to insist, strongly, that I marry a second time. The family was split right down the middle into two groups that refused to see eye to eye. Both tried to pull me over to their side. However, despite my mother's insistence, I refused to marry a second time. Finally, people began to cast aspersions on my sexual prowess and soon, all kinds of whispers began to circulate. I could not tolerate this and made up my mind to do something about it.

I went to my in-laws' house and said, 'Your daughter is not really ill. These are just false excuses to keep her here. I am going to take her with me.'

I told my wife as well, 'You are not really ill. At least not as ill as the people here have made you believe. All this is a hoax set up by your parents. It is not something that is hidden from you. You come and stay with me. Only then can we find out the truth about your illness.'

To begin with, she was a little bewildered by such blunt words but, after a bit of argument, she agreed to come away with me.

The two of us went on a long journey and then settled down in some remote hills. We often went out for long walks in the crisp, cool air.

After a span of time my wife recovered, and I took her home. It was a moment of pride for me when my friends and relatives saw the two of us together. However, a doubt still remained and they wanted foolproof evidence. I,

Masculinity

however, was fully confident of emerging victorious. Month after month passed—crawling at a snail's pace—and my wife's tummy became larger and larger.

My own state was like that of a gardener who overflows with contentment when he sees the seeds he's sown bear flowers. My victory became increasingly visible with every passing day, and with every passing moment. But my wife remained quiet. I thought that the reason for her nervousness was that of an expectant mother. Finally, the labour began. She was tortured and in pain for hours. Her body was tormented with unbearable agony and could not finding rest in any position. It seemed as if her very soul was begging for mercy. Her restlessness, her writhing, and her screams were the unmistakable proof of my virility.

❦

'Muazallah! God save me!' Her tortured screams still echo in my ears. The silence that fell after that—the silence which demolished my ego and my pride—I see it all clearly even now. But, after she passed on, people told me that she had died with a smile on her face. My heart was set at peace then, somewhat.

The Clouds Don't Come
~ Ahmed Ali ~

And the clouds don't come. The wretched clouds just won't come. God save us from this blazing heat. We're being roasted alive. We're being roasted, flapping like fish out of water. The incandescent sun and the intense heat! Even being baked in an oven cannot compare. This is hell. Have you ever suffered anything like it? If you haven't, taste it now. As far back as my memory can take me, I have never experienced such crazy, scorching heat. One simply gives up. The deer must be charred and blackened. Arre bhai, somebody speed up the fan. That will bring some relief at least.

A hush. Silence. Lethargy and stupor and trance and prance.

As children we had heard about a big cave in lap of the Himalayas. About how the flinty, thickly-forested peaks, which touch the skies, hid a huge, dark and deep den and how the mouth of the cave was stoppered by a huge rock. It was said that the clouds were locked away in this cave along with white, brown and black cows. Such foolish notions! Can there be any limit to ignorance? It is impossible to drive home a point however hard one tries! There's absolutely no discretion. Everybody has been cast in the same mould. Are we dogs that we should bark pointlessly? Nobody pays even the slightest attention. They've bid farewell to their senses. Arre, somebody must settle this question: which is mightier, the brain or brawn? Brawn, of course. A sturdy, brawny animal tethered by the flimsy cord of intelligence. Remain quiet and avoid the assault. Do moulvis have brains at all? Brains, intellect. And then taking pride in one's defects! The long beard hides the devious heart. They don't put their minds to work at all. They've abandoned common sense entirely. All they do is to pick up a book from some shelf, sit and read it, rhythmically rocking all the while. Bend low to read it. Wah! Well done! What mimicry! What senseless parroting! Wah mian! Go on, you parrot! Excellent mimicry! Well done! Read on! Keep repeating, Haq Allah, Paak zaat Allah, Paak Nabi Rasool Allah! Nabiji bhejo! Yah Allah bhej. Moulvi sahib, it's the child's desire, his strong desire. Who knows what sin I am being punished for? Don't worry, I am giving you two amulets. I don't believe in extolling my own virtues. I consider myself to be an insignificant, fallible creature of God. By the word of God, the will of God, may your wish be fulfilled. Read the namaaz of Esha, bathe, and

Angarey

then read the Darood Sharif seven times, fumigate these with incense and then tie one below your navel before having sex. Dissolve the other one in water and store it in a pot, add some water from the holy fountain of Mecca and drink the water first thing in the morning for seven successive days. God willing, your wish will certainly be granted. What? Is this your offering? Lahol vala quvata Illah-billah! Only God's grace can prevent a man from sinning, make him perform good deeds and drive away evil spirits. Are you not ashamed of yourself? Are you so presumptuous that you think that you can buy off the Word, the very discourse of God? Do you think that you can buy off God, too? I don't accept offerings, or any such thing. Go, give it to some juvenile humbug. Go. Get lost. Leave. Sir! It's my lapse, my fault. Do forgive me. Never again will I commit this blunder. Fine. I'll let it go this time but remember this one thing. An offering must be made to Bade Pir Sahibon on the night of the first Thursday after the new moon; and one rupee and a quarter, along with two hundred and fifty grams of jasmine flowers, must be offered on the tomb of Hare-Bhare Sahib. Qua ... a ... ari r-e—suaa aheb—a ... aa ... paki- dastaar-e-muba-a-rak ... yu ... baa ... aa .... rava mein ... kha ... tan ... ga ... aa ... aa.[3] Moulvi-sahib, did

---

[3]This is an attempt to reproduce the stretched-out sounds of rote learning. Here, for instance, the word 'quari', which is a special way of reading of the *Quran* in a guttural voice, the word is pronounced as 'qua a ari'. The idea of persistent repetition becoming absurd is

you eat it? Yes my child, I did. Moulvi-sahib, did you eat it? Yes my child, I did. No, Moulvi-sahib, tell me, did you really eat it? You pest! Did I not just say that I ate it? I ate it until I was more than full. May God destroy the English! They teach their language and turn everyone into atheists. It has made them impotent. It has brought such shame on masculinity. No one fears hell and no one desires heaven. All that was taught has been entirely forgotten. They poke fun at us. They ridicule Khuda-e-paak himself. They will come to their senses only when they have been scourged by fire. A hermit opens the mouth of that cave during the rains. The clouds roll out. Just listen, dear friend. Listen to these winged creatures; the birds, the insects—pankhi, mamoola, bulbul, podna and the taatal—making merry. Insects like the bhambhiri and titri. But the cat enters and all the fun is lost. Thud! Thud! All the merrymaking ends. You'll soon see what happens. May God grant us wisdom! It's true. The first signs of the Day of Judgement are to be clearly seen. The fire-spitting snake. Conflicts, battles, wars, the desecration of religion and of God. The world order is collapsing. These were the signs which heralded the collapse of ancient Greece. Oh God, have pity on us! These people are ignorant, uncouth. They know not what they say. You are the Lord of the universe. Pardon them.

Why won't the clouds come? Life is a hassle. A hassle... a ha ... hair ... long, black hair. A pointless burden. Why

---

communicated over the next few phrases.

Angarey

can't we just get it chopped off, like men do? I'm sure one's head must feel really light without hair. Abbajaan had only a few patches of hair on his head. Once, when it was as hot as this, he got the top of his head shaved clean off. Families have a strange concept of honour and reputation. If we chopped off our hair, it would be seen as no less than men chopping off their noses, bringing disrepute to their families. If I had been a boy, I would have chopped off their noses with a blunt knife—without even bothering to find a sharp one. Actually, I would have yanked their noses—the repository of all their reputation and honour—off. Then there would have been no fear of soiled reputations or chopped noses, for there would have been no noses to be chopped off anyway. Khuda does not give nails to the bald.

> Zakhm ke bharne tallak nakhun na badh aayenge kya?
> Zakhm bhar aaya par nakhoon hi nahin...

> Will the nails not grow until the wound scabs over?
> The wound is now scabbed, but I have no nails ...

Zakhm, a wound; raham, the womb; arrahimeen, the merciful. They all sound so similar, don't they? Was Khuda, too, made from a collection of wombs? Why are we born with wombs? Women have wretched lives, worse than the louse which sucks the blood from animals. Burdened with domestic chores, she's stitching, knitting, cooking, washing and cleaning all the time. She runs around from dawn to night, like a cat with scalded paws. And, to top it all, she bears children. It doesn't matter whether she wants it or not, her wretched husband pulls her close whenever he wants. Come here, my life, my love. Your coquetry brings such spice to life. There is such pleasure in your winning ways. See how cool, how serene, this room is. But you are the serenity of my heart, my life. Come here. Go away. The devil is always riding you. You don't care if it is night or day. Why don't you kill me? Run a knife through me. You've twisted my poor hand so hard. You've broken it! Why are you trying to run away? Come here, embrace me tightly, glue your body to mine. Come, taste the pleasure of being knifed. The wretched hands grope my breasts. They squash them with hard fingers. He's crushed them. The wretched one has pressed them so hard that I can't move at all. May this awful creature die young! No one must be treated like this, not even whores. But I was weak. What could I have done but lie down. All the heat, the fury, the raging passion, was spent on me. Why are you lying frozen, like a corpse? Don't you have any strength, some energy, some push? My beloved, my pyari, pi … aaa … ri, j … aaa … ni, my li … fff … ee. I, of course, can do nothing.

And why is it that I can do nothing? We would have refused to tolerate such humiliation if we had our own money. We would have done whatever we wished. But we don't even have the permission to earn money. All we can do is to rot behind the veil. Our lives are worse than that of those londis. Our position is much worse than that of animals. Caged.

Angarey

Imprisoned. With no room to even flutter our wings. What is our life, after all? We are entirely dependent on others. Like lamps, we have no control over when we are lighted and when we are snuffed out. But, of course, we are forever being charred. That is our fate. There is nothing else that destiny holds for us. And, on top of everything else, we have to be obedient, too. These worthless men merely wander about all the time. Sit somewhere with the hookah, or hang around elsewhere and gossip, play games or get busy with card tricks. Of course, the vile pack of cards is always waiting for them. And then, there's always the brothel to visit at night. The explanation offered is that they want to hear the women sing. But why, then, do they have to bathe so early the next morning? Why, then, discuss details and burn us up with jealousy. But what a pity, we don't even burn clean through. And though we shed endless tears, the wretched fire cannot be quenched. It rages all the time. Even death refuses to come to us—to end it all. The Hindus are better off. At least they have freedom. Of Christian women, of course, the less said the better. They simply do what they feel like. They dance, watch movies, get a haircut. They have been granted a destiny of calm and peace. It was in an ill-fated moment that we were born into a Muslim family. May such a religion go to hell! Religion.Religion? The real spirit of religion is contentment, the gratification of men. And none for the woman; she's insignificant. They grow a beard as wide as a palm and think of themselves as Muslims. They hunt from behind this bearded screen. As if we are not living. They ridicule us and make fun of our freedom. Abba-jaan had got us admitted into school after such great trouble. I'd barely reached the eight standard when—may God forgive his sins—he passed away. My name was withdrawn from the school and, soon, I was tied to this fat, bearded, burly brute. A real devil, he is. Forget about a woman's freedom, he is not willing to even to talk to her.

Have the oceans dried up that the clouds don't come? They've dried up. Even the oceans have dried up. Oceans. They came from across the seven seas. We were drowned too. We plunged in, we ducked. We're bathing in our own blood. The sun is really strong. It does not even turn to steam. From where will the steam come? The blood has dried up and turned to ash. But are the clouds really made of steam? We have heard that clouds are like sponges. They float in the air. When the heat is really intense, they come down to the shores of the ocean, gulp water, and then fly away. Perhaps they fear the government's navy. Perhaps they fear the cannons and dribble, trickle ... start pissing. Whatever they teach in schools is a lie. Clouds are not actually made of steam. All the geography they teach is entirely wrong. The terror of Imperial Britannia is the only real fact. Correct. That's it. Oh! It is only today, just now, at this moment, that I've finally understood it. What have you understood? The navy and the cannon. But the Afghan attacks in such a fantastic way. He hides behind boulders. As soon as he sees the enemy, he shuts one eye, perhaps both, presses the trigger and—bang! The living fall down—slump, slide, dribble—like a

Angarey

drop. What a shot! The Afghans walk about on the ground, but can bring down a flying plane with a single bullet. Forget a car, we don't even have a horse carriage. What can we do? We can visit the Jallianwala Bagh. But how will we travel? Should I really tell you how we should travel? Well then, in a wicker cart pulled by two oxen. Wah! Wah! Well said! So many people and a wicker cart. Crazy, absolutely crazy. Old age, you chaps. It's old age. Graying old age.Cut, chopped off. One way or the other—just chopped off. Hush, hush! Don't try and force yourself in! So, should we allow all of you to walk over our bodies! Crazy, absolutely crazy. Cut, chopped. That's the problem. He pays no attention. He completely ignores us. He just doesn't care. It is like water running off a duck's back! He rolls around in the mud. He doesn't even care about what he looks like. What was the couplet? What was it?

Hamne apni surat bigad li,
unko tasveer banna aati hai,

I'm now hideous
But you, of course, look good

What was it? What was it?

Ek hum hain, hain hum.

I am the one who doesn't care about what I look like.

Black, dirty, half-naked, unconcerned. Ready for a fight at the slightest provocation from kith and kin. And the others are unjust. No one seems to care about that. Get beaten, shoed, abused and, then, the same frivolity of youngsters. Just dare strike me and see what I'll do. Well, then, here's a slap. Okay, but if you hit just one more time—slap, slap; bawl, bawl! Look, Amma, Chunnu just doesn't listen to me. He keeps slapping me. Talk some sense into him or else this bastard— Mashallah! Chashme baddoor! May you be saved from the evil eye! What sweet abuse. Kiss him, kiss him. I'll pull your tongue out of the nape of your neck. I'll slap you so hard that all this vulgarity will end once and for all. Beats one like a dog. First entices with a bone and then strikes. Calls one close first, and then hits. Hems one in, and then beats; loves and beats; pampers and beats; forget other things, beats, and then beats. And we, like dogs, after going through all this, lick their bottoms once more. The regret is that we don't even get the shit. Ah thoo! Scrape the tongue. The shit of a black dog! Shame on people like you. So, is it over? Finished? Have you managed to tolerate Chunnu's abuse? Beat him. Beat him. What are you waiting for? Leap up and strike him. Beat him up. We march to hunt the elephant, behind our chief who has just crushed a fly. Try and understand what you really are—utterly insignificant! Well done, my braggart—the sheer pretence of courage. Wah! It deserves a comment. An honest comment. Hum bair basavan jayein—we march into battle. It would have made some sense if you had said ber, or berries, and not bair. Mian, the bers

Angarey

from Sheikhupura are really good. Have you ever heard of bers from Saharanpur? Hazrat, it must be bael, the ox. Yes, absolutely correct. Ox, of course. Hum bair basavan jayein. A wicker-cart pulled by two oxen—and?—Raja mari podani hum bair basavan jayein. Wah mian, podani ... what courage you've shown. A paper tiger? We will sit in a wicker-cart, ox. Our chief has just crushed a fly, and we march behind him to hunt an elephant.

A Night of Winter Rain
~ Ahmed Ali ~

Garrrad! Garrrad! Garrrad! Eilahi khair! God save us! It looks like the sky will crack open today. Has a roof collapsed somewhere?

All at once, the cracks in the doors were lighted up by a jagged dazzle and a strong gust of wind shook the whole house. Brrr, it's freezing! My body shivers so intensely that my very bones might break.

A room, twenty-four feet by twenty-four feet in size, of which more than half is taken over by a narrow verandah. Behind it is another tiny, dark room with a low roof. The room in front does not have a proper floor. Some ragged old pieces of jute, clammy with moisture, have been spread out on the floor. A heap of dirty bags and chunks of used cotton are stacked in the corners. Clay pots which have become black and have been reduced to half their original

Angarey

size due to repeated use over long years are spread over a solitary, broken wooden box. There is a single copper pot amongst these. Its edges are now worn out. The pot has not been polished for years and long scrubbing has thinned its base so that it is about to give way.

The ceiling has disappeared and, now, only the wooden beams are visible in its place. And the rain on top of everything. Allah! Will the winter rain, this mahavatt, really come down so fiercely this year? Like it did last year? Stop now, at least. Where should I go? What can I do? It is better to die. Why did you make me poor? Either that or you should not have shown me better days. This house is in such a wretched condition that there is no space to even lie down. The roof is leaking like a sieve and though, like a kitten, I've explored all corners for a dry spot, I can't find any. There is no respite. It doesn't matter so much to me; it is the children who will be affected. How can one ever sleep like this? And, worse, we have just one quilt for four people. Have mercy, Allah. There was a time when we had palaces and carpets, servants and bedsteads. My room, ah! A high, royal bed with golden coverlets; velvet sheets and pillows of soft cotton. My mattress, so soft that one fell asleep as soon as one lay on it. The printed silk quilts with golden borders. The numerous maids who milled about, pestering me with questions. 'Biwi, should I massage your head? Your feet?' One oiled my hair, another kneaded my hands. That soft, yielding bed and all that pampering! Sleep, dressed in a garment of stars, waiting... Blue, red and purple images

A Night of Winter Rain

on green window panes. Glittering precious stones... Shining silver plates and the dastarkhwan with its delicacies—the korma, the pulao, the biryani, the mutanjan, the baaquarkhaani, the meethe tukde. A garden ringed by trees, their dark green leaves aglow with starlight reflected in drops of dew. Mango, the king of fruits—a mother's pampered child. And apples so pleasing to the eye. The fruits, crimson, pink and pale green, bend the boughs with their weight. Look at these fleshy berries, how plump and red they are. They are from Sheikhupura. A stream, a silver sheet on a dark night—or is it milk? Could this be heaven? A boat floating like a graceful swan. Quick, board it and go to heaven. What beautiful women, fair, pristine like clear crystal, like transparent glass, dressed in pure white. Elegant, like the wind. The boat moves on water like a lighted lamp. The open fields on either banks are covered with green grass, punctuated by fruit trees and rows of colourful flowers. The birds sing; such a racket! Is this heaven? Are we in heaven? Yes. The place where all of Khuda's good and benevolent people end up. The boat floated by some houses with domes shining like seashells. What beauty and brilliance! The dazzle is blinding. So, do these houses leak, too? No, certainly not. Can I find a place in them? It is a place for the compassionate and virtuous people of God. The pure ones! There is an itch inside my stomach and a tug at my heart; the intestines turn inside out. It felt like somebody had placed something on my lap. It was a fruit—as large as an apple and white like a pearl. There were two green

Angarey

leaves, too, attached to the stem. It seemed like it had just been plucked from the branch. Aha, wonderful! Alas, there should have been more. My lap was overloaded. The boat was sailing in-between two hills. We approached a bend and the boat turned swiftly. All at once, flames shot up from a tall mountain in the distance, brighter than lightning itself. The unbearable glare dazzled my eyes. After the blaze, the darkness was impenetrable. Then, I heard a sound louder than any thunder. It was the soor, the devastating sound produced by the angel Israfeil on the Day of Judgement—so loud that it drowned everything else. The women on the boat ran helter-skelter. Just then, there was a massive eruption of light—the sun was falling! Then, nearby, an explosion took place with the violence of an erupting volcano. The boat overturned and it looked like everyone would drown.

Garrad! Garrad! Tup, tup! The sound engulfed us from all directions. Amma! Amma! There was still some hearing left in my ears. My heart was palpating. What is it, son? What is it? I am frightened! What was that sound? Nothing, my son. It's the thunder. The three children had shrunk into a corner. The water which had leaked in had reached their quilt. The corner of the quilt which covered Mariam was completely wet—poor thing. She got up and shifted the children further away. They were now squeezed against the wall. Ya Allah, if the roof continues to leak like this, then all of us are certain to be wet. Amma, I am cold. Siddiqua was lying next to her. She embraced her even more tightly. The quilt and the embrace—double the warmth. There, the

A Night of Winter Rain

two boys were lying down entwined with each other—like a snake coiled around a tree.

Ya Allah, have pity! Khuda stays with the poor, helps them and pays heed to their sighs. Is He there at all? Who— What is He, after all? Whatever He is, he is so cruel! So unjust! Why is one rich and the other poor? It is His strategy. What strategy! Someone lies in the cold without even a bed to sleep on. With nothing to cover himself with. So... Bear the cold, the rain, the hunger. Even death does not come easily to such people. And then there are the others who have lakhs of rupees, all kinds of things, and lack for nothing. What will they lose if they give a bit of what they have to us too? The poor would manage to survive on the little that they get. But why should they care? Why should they feel responsible for people like us? Who created us? Allah. So why does He not care about us? Why did He create us after all? Just for us to bear all this sorrow and trouble? What injustice! Why are they rich and we aren't? All this will be avenged on the Day of Judgement. At least that's what the moulvis say. The Day of Judgement? It can go to hell! Our need, our pain is now, in the present. The fever is raging now, at this precise point in time, but the medicine will be administered after a decade. Enough about the Day of Judgement! We will tackle it when we come to it, but what about now? This very instant, when something needs to be done? Khuda—an excuse, a mere deception! The consolation of being poor. The consolation of holding on to hope in the state of despair! The acceptance of pain during troubled

Angarey

times. Khuda—an excrescence of deception. And it is religion which instills this in us. Which teaches us exactly this. And it is this which is called the treasure of knowledge. Actually, it is an excuse for poverty. Camouflaged as sense for the foolish, it is the sense of the foolish which pulls down the person who is trying to move up in life. A hurdle in the path of progress. Remain poor; it is only through poverty that one can reach God. We haven't received anything yet. Why does He not take some money for us from the rich? We don't want too much, just enough to get through life. What do the rich do with money anyway? It lies useless and unused with them. They don't know how to spend it. It's spent irrationally, and wasted Why does the government not do anything about it? If nothing else, then at least the money could be divided equally amongst all. If pushed still further, we could make do with even half the portion. But why should the government care? Its own treasury is overflowing. It collects money without ever moving even the little finger. Why should it bother anyone at all? We are the ones who are in trouble. Only the one who wears the shoe knows where and how hard it bites. However ...

Amma. Yes, my son. What is it? Amma, I am hungry. Hungry. A tremor ran through Mariam's body. Ya Eilahi! What should I do? Poor children! Mian, is this the time to feel hungry? Are you sure it is hunger and not some other craziness? Go to sleep, you'll get food in the morning. No, Amma, I want food just now, I am really hungry. No, son, not at this time. Just lie down. Listen, just listen to the thunder. The child, poor thing, was frightened by the loud thunder and lay down in fear. From where can I get food? What should I do? The rain has not allowed me to step out. I have not been able to go to anybody's house to fetch whatever little they may have possibly given. I could not even manage to go to dear Faiyyaz-begum. She is a dear and gives away whatever leftovers she possibly can. What will happen if I cannot find work tomorrow, too? How long can I beg for? People must be getting fed up of giving alms.

Amma, I'm hungry. Just see how empty my stomach is. I haven't eaten anything since yesterday morning. I can't sleep like this. My heart is sinking. Poor thing, she finally got up and rummaged about. She went to the box, hoping to find something to give to the child. He's a mere five-year-old. I wish I had not given them birth. I would have gone through my life one way or the other, but it's unbearable to see them in pain. She finally found a dried-up roti in a clay pot. She broke it into pieces, soaked it in water and brought it to the child. Hunger makes one desperate. He attacked the roti like a dog. After eating a bit he said, Amma, give me some jaggery if you can find some. Mariam stood up again wondering if she could possibly lay her hands on a small piece of jaggery. Incidentally, she did find a small lump. The child ate whatever he could. Mariam could not stop herself, picked up the leftovers and ate them.

The lightning and thunder had stopped. The rain, too, had abated. She once again embraced Siddiqua and lay down. Now she was alone again.

Angarey

Ah, I wish he was here. He. He. He! He would come back home at night with something or the other. What have you got? Halwa soan. The wretched thing must have dried up by now. You know that I like habshi halwa better. Look here, you've started screaming again. At least have a look at it. Ah, those quarrels and those reconciliations. The coming together of contraries, the co-existence of different seasons at the same time. Those were amazing days indeed! They are like dreams beyond reach now. And, then, the phoolwalon ki sair, the festival of flowers, on moonlit nights. Ah, that bed! Its mere fragrance could drive one mad. Now, even the stale flowers have vanished. I wish he was here. Those legs, like straight tree trunks, of bone, marrow and flesh, its sap much warmer than even blood; its skin much softer than flesh. One trunk, straight and strong with two branches; two branches, two souls and a single trunk. Entwined with each other; stuck to each other; each others' soul; joined, entwined, each carrying the others' life and together in the hope of a third soul—the treasure of a full, complete life. The wealth of that single moment! The evidence of existence in non-existence! Ah, those legs! Two snakes coiled together, lying intoxicated on the grass wet with dew. A threaded needle and two fingers—swiftly moving, galloping—are tracing out shapes on the soft velvet mattress. A spider, in its usual spot, is weaving a web. Moving up and down, it doesn't realize that the fly is already trapped; and the glue continues to be stretched into wires, weaving webs. A pot hangs down in the depths of a well. It touches its bottom, feels the warmth of its soft sand. Small circles on the surface of water spread out till they cover it fully, striking against the walls. They ripple out and ripple back. A sensation of warmth suffuses everything. Two twin trees—mango and pipal—growing out of the same root, engendered from the same trunk, confidants of a single life, grew together; they're each other's support, they console each other. Survivors from the same source! Ah, that body! And now the pipal has been blighted by lightning. But I—the unfortunate mango tree—still live on. I wish it was I who had been struck by lightning, left leafless, alone, dried up. You parasite! You still continue to live. Only if he had been alive!

A movement under the quilt—Siddiqua turns.

Ah, time cannot be deceived. It cannot be coaxed. And I, alone. It would have been easier if I had not seen better days. I would not have felt such intense loneliness if I didn't know. There would have been no empty space in my heart—that space for love. Hope can move through such heights and depths. At times it seems so close and so far off at other times. But there's nothing left to hope for anyway. Now all that exists is deep despair. It envelops everything, shrouds everything like a cloud. That swing hanging from white, cotton ropes. Four companions—two on each edge of the wooden plank—the mounting swing shakes the tree, touches and then enters the clouds, moving with the rhythms of the song, 'Jhoola kinne dalo re, aa moraiyan'. Wah, Anwari and Kishwar, my dear friends, is that as high as you can push the swing? Just see how high Kubra and I can go. I bet your head would reel if you as much as looked at us; then, a ripple of laughter. Ah, those times seem like a sheer illusion now. The houris' pleasant sojourns. No more the garland of flowers, the swing of dew drops, the branch of the ber tree. Where then can I hope to find some refuge? Once again, a hot rocky tract, infertile and hard—and life beside it—but, then, a new life. Renewed dignity once again—the sheer delight of man-vasalva, the undeserved manna from heaven; nay, heaven itself. Frolicking in rivers of sweetened milk. And then all days will be as pleasurable as Eid and nights as Shab-e-Barat. But ah, a change in fortune—Satan and the fall for having tasted wheat—and destruction, and loneliness, loneliness, loneliness! A mountain of misfortune! Oh, Adam, the pain, the problems, the humiliation, the hardships—and then, once again, the same joy, destruction all around. Self-centredness, the deafening sound Israfeil makes. And Dajjal, the evil one, trying to mislead us all. I will go to him—ah, this loneliness, there's no one to caress me, or place a soothing hand on my head. Neither satisfaction, nor consolation, nor solace—loneliness, loneliness! A dark and terrifying night! 'La do koi jangal mujhe ... jungle ... mujhe ... bazaar ... ba ... zaar ... mod ...' aoujh, I ask for the impossible!

Night.

Behind the Veil:
A One-Act Play
~ Rashid Jahan ~

[A room with white flooring. A mattress is spread in the centre of the room. A woman, lying back on bolsters, is seated on the mattress. She looks sad and tired. Next to her is a surahi, containing water, which is placed upon a silver plate with its mouth covered with a small metal bowl. Seated in front of her is another woman who looks to be near forty. She is slicing betel nuts. On one side lies a round box and, on the other, a spittoon. The room has two doors in front. The walls around have many cupboards, shelves and ledges with different objects such as kitchen utensils, lids and covers. A cloth fan with a pink frill is hanging from the middle of the ceiling. A bedstead with a coverlet spread on it is visible in one corner of the room. At the other end is another mattress with a bolster and a spittoon next to it.]

Mohammadi-begum: Aapa, who is bothered about us anyway? We have already lived most of our lives and Allah will see to the rest. I am so fed up and sick of this world that I would have poisoned myself if I was not concerned about these little children.

Aftab-begum: Have you gone mad, bua, my dear lady? This is hardly the age to talk of poison and of suicide. It is only now that spring has blossomed for you. The children, with God's grace, are grown up. How can the idea of poisoning yourself even come to you? Just look at me ...

Mohammadi-begum: Why should I look at you? Do you think this has anything to do with age? Is it only the old who get weary of the world? The lust for life that I have seen in the old is hardly to be matched by the young. Death comes to so many people—God only knows where my death has gone and hidden itself. Everybody—including children—forgets everything after a while and life comes back on track soon after that ...

Aftab-begum: Get a grip, my dear, get a grip! You are still too young to plead for death. You are a decade or so younger to me. They were talking about my marriage in the year that you were born. That was the year when the queen died. I remember it very well. May her soul find peace. Chachi

Behind the Veil: A One-Act Play

amma was so happy. 'She's like a son for me,' she used to say about you. You were born almost thirty years after chachi amma's marriage. What celebrations! There was eating and drinking; and the Dom women danced their special dance. Not just that, your marriage, too, was solemnized with such great fanfare. The whole city of Dilli went into raptures over it. Who could be as fortunate as you? Look at how unfortunate I am. Allah bless you, you have a husband, children, home, everything.

Mohammadi-begum: Yes, that's true. Husband, children, a home; I have it all. Youth? Who will call me young? I look like an old woman of seventy. This unending illness; the daily visits by hakims and doctors. And a child every year! Yes, of course, who can be more fortunate than I am? [Her eyes fill with tears. She wipes her eyes with a handkerchief and, after spitting into the spittoon, she begins to speak once again.] It just happened two months ago. It was decided that the lady doctor be called just before the miscarriage. Doctor Ghayas's diagnosis also pointed to the fact that my ongoing fever may be due to some internal disorder. He felt that it would be better to get an internal check-up done by the lady doctor. And as far as the ageing is concerned, you must listen to this. The lady doctor asked me my age. 'Thirty-two years,' I said. She smiled in a way that gave me the impression that she did not believe me. I said, 'Miss sahib, why are you smiling? You should know that I got married when I was seventeen. And since then I have borne a child every year, except when my husband went abroad for a year. And the second time such a thing happened was when he and I had quarrelled. These teeth that you see missing have been pulled out by Dr Ghayas. Some pyorrhoea or something like that—God knows what disease it is—that's what has happened. The whole problem was that when my dear husband returned from his trip abroad, he began to complain that my mouth smelled bad.' The poor lady doctor, what could she do? She just laughed.

Aftab-begum: You say such absurd things! What can people do but laugh?

Mohammadi-begum: Anyway, the lady doctor did check my stomach and my chest. Then when she did an internal check-up, she got really nervous and said, 'Begum sahiba. It looks like you are pregnant again. It has been two months.' My heart missed a beat! Another problem to confront now! [Just then, the sound of some children weeping and others shrieking and screaming is heard from the other room. Begum sahiba, who has been resting with her back on the bolster, straightens up and yells.] Arre, you ruffians! There isn't a moment of peace here. We keep so many haramzaadi maids but the children make a racket all the time. It would be better if God just ended my life and freed me of this world's problems. [The door opens. Two maids, dressed in clean clothes, enter with two weeping children. Some other, older, children are seen standing at the door. All the children

Behind the Veil: A One-Act Play

are thin, pale and underweight. The inner courtyard is now visible through the open door.]

First maid: Begum-sahiba, Nahne-mian does not listen to me at all. Whenever he enters the room, he starts troubling all the other children. He doesn't let them play. Now he has run away with Nanhi-bi's doll and Chote-mian's ball. And he has run into the the men's rooms.

Mohammadi-begum: [In anger] He's a butcher, the scoundrel, a butcher! He leaves nobody in peace in the house. Like father like son! [She picks up the child and comforts her. She then takes something out of the box and gives it to both the children to eat.] Go, for God's sake, leave now. All I get to hear from morning to evening is just shrieking and screaming. [Then, after a pause, seeing that the maid has left the door ajar, she says] Arre! Shut the door at least. I have said the same thing so many times since morning! Whenever they go out of the room, they just leave the door open.

Aftab-begum: Bua, the wretched doctor attends to your family at all times. Even so, look at the children. They're so thin, pale, stunted and undernourished.

Mohammadi-begum: How else can they be when they are deprived of their mother's milk? They bring home any kind of wet nurse they can find; the blind, the pock-marked, the

Angarey

fat, the thin. Whoever one stumbles upon is employed. My husband is the decision-maker. He says that I need not bother with all this when, with God's grace, we have the money. As far as he is concerned, all pleasure is limited to his own lust. His only worry is that he will be inconvenienced if a child stays with me. He is not concerned, be it night or day. All he wants is for his wife to be available to him at all times. And, of course, he does not stop at his wife. There is absolutely no holding him back from going to other places too.

Aftab-begum: Mohammadi-begum, you blame your poor husband for everything. If he employs maids he becomes a villain and if he doesn't, he is a scoundrel. Bua, chant Allah's name.

Mohammadi-begum: Aapa, you weren't here when Nasir died. The poor boy was just four months old. May Allah not let even our enemies suffer the way he did; even strangers could not bear to see his pain. His wet nurse looked quite hefty and tall but carried some disease which heated up her insides. Now how could anyone have known about that? As a result, the child exploded with sores. His whole body was covered with blisters. Raw flesh would squirt out when the blisters burst. All his joints were filled with pus. Doctor Ghayas used to drain out pots full of pus—I used to watch from behind the curtain. 'Don't even breathe,' he'd say, 'just thank your stars.' After all this, the child festered for two months before he bid his final farewell. I have borne

Behind the Veil: A One-Act Play

three children after that. I insisted so much upon feeding them myself but who cares? I am always terrorized by the threat, 'I will remarry if you breastfeed the children. I need a woman at all times. I don't have the patience to wait while you attend to the children.' And then you say ...

Aftab-begum: So, that's the problem! How was I to know all this? God save us from such men; even animals have some restraint. This behaviour is worse than that of animals. May one be saved from such men! Such things didn't happen earlier, bua. These days, all the men you see, wretched burly bullies, have the same problem. Now look at my husband, your own brother-in-law. He is old now but he avoided all excesses even as a young man. [Smiling] I swear by God, I made him lick my feet for hours.

Mohammadi-begum: [Sighing] To each her own fate! What you just said has reminded me that the story of my conversation with the lady doctor is still not over. Words have a strange way of changing track. So then, after saying that I was two months pregnant, the lady doctor stared at me with surprise, 'Begum-sahiba, you were saying that you have been bedridden for the last four months and that you get fever every evening. And Dr Ghayas, too, said that you get hundred or a hundred-and-one fever every evening. So then, do you mean ...?' I said, 'Aye, Miss sahib! You are fortunate. You earn money for yourself, you spend it the way you wish to, and sleep in peace. As far as I am concerned,

Angarey

who cares if I go to hell or to heaven! All that they care about is their pleasure and enjoyment. The wretched wife may live or die, all that men hunger after is their own lust. The lady doctor, poor thing, just heard me out and kept quiet. Then she said, 'You are so very ill,' and bua, not just this doctor but all the other doctors also say that the children can't be healthy when I am so weak myself. And to make matters worse, the children keep coming so close to each other. Anyway, what can one do? It would have been better to have been born a Christian.

Aftab-begum: Tauba, tauba, don't utter such blasphemies! I have just one son and even he has kept a Christian woman. I had such dreams for his marriage. My brother, in frustration, has now gone and settled Waheeda's marriage somewhere else. Just imagine how my heart wrenches with anguish to know that the girl I had asked for since she was a child is now going to a stranger's home. It would have been better if he had never been born. He is as good as dead for me now.

Mohammadi-begum: How can you curse him so? He is the support of your old age, after all. He will certainly reform sooner or later.

Aftab-begum: What reform? He will never reform! It has been two years. I have yearned for him for so long, but haven't had the merest glimpse of him. He stays in this very

Behind the Veil: A One-Act Play

city but has not stepped into the house even once. I hear he earns one hundred and fifty rupees now. And thank God, at least there is no child yet. I have only one prayer now. Even if I am left with no one to light a lamp on my grave, his wife, that haramzaadi, may she die in the bloom of her youth and never ever bear a child! Bua, who can we share our pain with? Each one of us is weighed down with our own misfortunes. Mohammadi-begum, did you hear this other news? Mirza Maqbool Ali Shah has just married again. Two wives have already died and even his granddaughters have children. And this latest wife of his is so young; with such an innocent face! She would hardly be twenty. The unlucky girl is doomed. She has six unmarried sisters. That's why the poor parents... [The twelve-year-old elder son, the lower ends of his pyjamas covered with grime, pushes the door open and runs in. He has a spool of thread in one hand and a pair of scissors in the other. Behind him enters a strong-looking girl wearing tight pyjamas.]

Girl: Amma, Bade-mirza just won't listen. See how he has put cuts in my new pyjamas. [Saying this, she lifts up her kurta and shows it to her mother.] I was not even talking to him. I was just putting buttons on Abbajan's achkan. And look here, he has even torn my dupatta. [Frustrated, she leans against the wall and starts weeping.]

The boy: [Imitating his sister] Ouh, ouh, ouh. You are not saying anything about what you were really doing. So, you were sewing? Were you? Should I tell Amma what vulgar books you were reading? *Dildaar Yaar? Baanka Chhabila?*

Girl: [Turning towards him] For God's sake, don't lie! I swear by God, Amma, I was reading Moulvi Ashraf Ali Sahab's *Bahishti Zevar*. He started pestering me to show it to him. When I didn't, he just slashed my pyjamas. You never say anything to him.

Mohammadi-begum: [Smacking her forehead] Shabash beti! Amma may live or die, but it never crosses your mind that you should help her. Instead, you end up quarrelling with your younger brothers. [Then, turning towards her son] This rowdy creature keeps troubling someone or the other all the time. Get lost!

Aftab-begum: Come, mian, give me the scissors. Do you know of anybody else who troubles his sister like this? After all, she is with you only for a short time. She will get married and go away in a year or two. After that, however much you may yearn, you will not get even a small glimpse of her. [Sabira, embarrassed with this talk, bends her head and quietly slips away. Bade Mirza rides on the bolster as if it were a horse and begins to jump up and down after a few moments.]

The boy: So why did she not show me the book then?

Behind the Veil: A One-Act Play

Mohammadi-begum: Bade-mirza, have pity for God's sake! Don't shake me up like this. My whole body is trembling. My heart has begun to throb so hard. For God's sake, go out to your abba. Moulvi-sahib must be about to come. Have you finished your lessons? [The mere mention of studies makes Bade Mirza feel that it would be better for him to go away.]

Aftab-begum: The house at least looks full when there are so many children. But the noise and the commotion can get on one's nerves. Bua, now I just stay at home all day, idle and twiddling my thumbs. My husband comes in only for namaaz. He sits for a moment or two and then goes back to the sitting room. May God never make anyone as lonely as me. What dreams I had! [The door opens and Kolan, an old maid, enters, holding something in her hands.]

Kolan: Salaam, Begum-sahib. Salaam, Badi-begum. Here, take this. I was about to go to your house with your portion. So begum, how are you? How are the children?

Mohammadi-begum: Well, bua, I am surviving. I hope bhabhi is fine. And the kids, I hope they are fine too. My best wishes for the new grandson. This must be the panjiri. Rahiman, here, take this and empty the plate. [She opens the small box.] Aapa, please hand me a paan.

Aftab-begum: Rahiman, just take my share too. [Saying

Angarey

this, she gets busy preparing paan. Mohammadi gives two annas to Kolan.]

Mohammadi-begum: Convey my regards to everybody. I will come as soon as I feel a little better. Meeting you has renewed my desire to meet everybody once again. I really feel like seeing the baby. And bua, just ask bhabhi if she has sworn never to come here? [Aftab hands the paan over and, taking out some money from her waistband, gives two annas to Kolan.]

Kolan: Begum-sahiba, my bibi, too, remembers you a lot but she hardly finds any spare time. These days, of course, the house is full. Everybody has come.

Aftab-begum: Convey my blessings to Sultan-dulhan. And my congratulations on the grandson. God willing, I will come on this Friday. [Kolan takes the two plates, offers her salaam, and leaves.]

Mohammadi-begum: Aapa, our bhabhi Sultan has her own special style. Her mian never earned more than forty rupees but she has such a talent that she has managed to do everything really well within her limited means. She got her sons and daughters married off. Now, with God's grace, her son has found a good job and earns something around a hundred and fifteen. There's also scope for promotion.

Behind the Veil: A One-Act Play

Aftab-begum: The daughter-in-law is good, too. [Sighs] It's fate. Look at us. Anyway, forget it. Is there any news of Razia? Your mamu got her engaged and married off in such haste that he hardly invited anybody.

Mohammadi-begum: So what if he did not invite people? He got food and delicacies distributed twice or thrice amongst all the families. The poor girl got married under such circumstances ... in the fear of disgrace. Still, may God bless them all.

Aftab-begum: Was that it? I had no idea! So what happened?

Mohammadi-begum: Really? You really don't know? Everybody seems to know about it now. The poor thing is so young. She's just about two years older than my Sabira. She was born after I got married. When Chote-mamu came from Calcutta—he had come after many years—all of us were quite young at that time. Nani-amma, poor thing, even with her trembling limbs, was the happiest of all. I had brought Razia home with me for a few days. Then Choti-mami went to her parents' house. The girl stayed over with me for three or four months. Razia is so fond of her father's family that she can give her life for them. She is not so attached to her mother's side of the family. This is my house, her cousin sister's house but I had not the slightest inkling of what was happening. Razia went back when her mother returned from her parents' home. One day a terse note from Razia

Angarey

arrived, saying, 'Aapa-jaan, for God's sake, hurry up and come here.' That's it Aapa, what can I say? When I reached her house, then Choti-mami ... you do know Choti-mami, don't you? You know how she can pretend to be very sweet. So, she welcomed me profusely. Razia handed me a letter in secret and said, 'Dulhe-bhai, your husband, comes here every day and Amma showers great attention and care on him in secret. They talk softly in secret.' Poor, young, unwed girl! What more could she have said? She had gathered all her courage to say even as much as she did. And the letter—it was my mian's letter to Razia. A kind of love letter that is impossible to find even in romantic novels. I literally burnt up with anger. I talked to Razia and convinced her that her name will not be implicated. I came back home smouldering. I discussed the matter with my mian. Aye aapa, I swear by God, he was so shameless that he didn't even blink his eyes. 'So, what's the harm?' he said, 'I will marry Razia. Even if it means a talaq from you.' I said, 'Are you in your senses or have you bid goodbye to them? She is from a respectable family. Even if you as much as utter her name, her father, brothers and uncles will chop you to pieces. Don't even dream of anything as far as she is concerned.'

Aftab-begum: So, your mumani had fixed everything on the sly.

Mohammadi-begum: What else? She has nursed some deep grudge against Amma and me for long. Even when

Behind the Veil: A One-Act Play

Amma was ill, she used to swear that she would not be at peace till she ruins my home. And it is not that she has this animosity only towards us. She has a similar grudge against elder mumani too. And since Razia was engaged to a boy in my chacha's family, she constantly fought about it, saying that she would never give away her daughter into the family of her enemies.

Aftab-begum: [Laughing] And bua, what is attractive about your mian anyway? He has a wife and children; except, of course, that he has money. But then your elder mamun, too, is not poor. Do such things ever happen in respectable families? I have heard that in some places far off in the west, two sisters may wed their daughters to the same man but it doesn't happen in our families. But, of course, these are modern times. It seems that anything can happen now. So then, what happened next?

Mohammadi-begum: When I lost my cool and said bitter things to him, he began to cajole me and said, 'Believe me, I am completely smitten with her. For God's sake, help me. It is your duty to help me.' He used to sit with the *Quran Sharif* and read out aayats about the kind of hell I will face after death if I don't help my husband. Anyway, which fire could have burnt me more than the one I carried within me, the one which scorched me all the time? In short, the same story that he would go mad was repeated endlessly. He confined himself to a room, lying all the time with his face

Angarey

buried in the bed and all he chanted was, 'Hai Razia, hai Razia.' And I had little choice but to quietly listen to this. I swear by God, Aapa, my heart is so deeply plagued by all this that all wealth and luxury have become a burden to me. I'd rather live poorly on dry roti if I could only get a little happiness. Aapa, just hand me a paan. My mouth has become parched from all the speaking. [She drinks water from the surahi. Aftab takes out a paan for herself and hands one to Mohammadi, too.] In short, this situation remained unchanged. He kept saying such vulgar and lustful things about that poor unmarried child. I felt completely stifled but could hardly do anything besides listening quietly to all this. And as far as choti mumani is concerned, she continued to behave in the same way, greeting and welcoming him with the same warmth. 'Razia,' she would say, 'your dulha bhai is here. Give him some paan and elaichi.'

Aftab-begum: Achha! What is certain is that all this was hatched by your mumani.

Mohammadi-begum: Of course! What else? That girl used to weep for hours. She expressed her agony and unburdened her heart to me whenever we met. I kept quiet for a month. Then both my mamus came to meet me. I then asked them, 'Mamu jaan, has Razia's engagement been called off?' Both the brothers were bewildered. I was, of course, already full of all this to the brim and divulged everything to them. After that, both of them must have considered and deliberated

Behind the Veil: A One-Act Play

upon the matter and the result was that Razia was married off on the third day.

Aftab-begum: Allah, Allah, khair salla! All's well that ends well.

Mohammadi-begum: But bua, he did not enter the house for six months. He just spent all his time with those whores in Chaawadi. And I was happy. God knows, I sleep in peace on days when he goes there. Now the same story is repeated every day. He keeps saying, 'You keep ill. How long do you expect me to go through all this? I have decided to remarry.' And to top it all he also insists, 'You are the one who will have to arrange my marriage. When Islamic law allows four marriages, then why should I not remarry?' I said, 'Go ahead. Sabira will be married off after a year. Father and daughter can marry at the same time. On the one hand play with the grandson and with your new wife's child on the other. That's it! He immediately starts quarrelling, 'What do women know about all this. God has not gifted them with passions that we have.' I just say to him that, actually, he has within him the concentrated passions of all men put together....

Aftab-begum: [Interrupting] Mohammadi-begum, wherever you go, you will find the same problem. Men seem to have their way all along. They triumph in all situations—tails they win, heads we lose. Now tell me, isn't it bad enough to say, 'I will remarry,' that he also insists that, 'my wife is the one

Angarey

who must arrange it!'

Mohammadi-begum: That's the reason why I am in deep distress and pray for death to end my life. My own health is a big problem and the problems with the children make matters worse. The older children, God save them, are quite healthy but the younger ones are never well. All this has destroyed my desire to live. And the fear of his second marriage haunts me at all times. Khuda, bring death to me before he brings home another woman. And what all have I not done because of this fear of the other woman? I've undergone two surgeries.

Aftab-begum: What we had heard was that you had got something done to put a stop to children from being born.

Mohammadi-begum: Who told you all this? The real reason was that my uterus as well as my lower parts had begun to slide down. It needed to be corrected so that my mian could get the pleasure of a new wife from my body. Bua, how long can the body of a woman who produces children year after year remain fit? It slipped down again. Then once again I was slaughtered with force and threat. But despite all this, he is still unhappy. [The azaan is called from a mosque close by.]

Aftab-begum: Bua, it's time for the afternoon namaaz. I got so engrossed with chatting that I just forgot about everything else. [She ties a cloth over her head and torso.] Now I will go only after namaaz. Your brother, poor thing, will be waiting.

Mohammadi-begum: Aapa, thank God you came today. I could at least unburden myself. Do keep coming more often. I am ill and just can't go out. [She then calls out, 'Rahiman, Rahiman, Gulshaboo!' Rahiman appears.]

Mohammadi-begum: Go help Badi-begum with her wuzoo.

CURTAIN DROPS

Acknowledgements

We were extremely circumspect and uncertain when we started translating *Angarey* into English. The original Urdu text combines the complexity of a narrative technique like the stream of consciousness with multilayered political, religious, literary and social connotations. It all started with an informal talk regarding the beginnings of progressive writers and writing in the India of early 1930s which gradually matured into a fascination that eventually saw its culmination in this translation. We stole time between classes and worked in the library of our college, Zakir Husain Delhi College, to complete this project.

Our heartfelt thanks are due to Nadira Z. Babbar who was extremely enthusiastic about our work from the moment we discussed it with her over the phone. She was also generous enough to write the foreword to this edition. Despite her extremely busy schedule, filled to capacity with

Angarey

writing, directing and acting in theatre and films, she made it a point to give us the foreword well in time. This brings to the book a personal element without which it would have been quite incomplete.

This translation would not have been possible without the whole-hearted support of late Qamar Rais in the compilation and publication of the Urdu edition of *Angarey* in 1995. It is with heartfelt gratitude that we also remember late Nikhat Kazmi for her erudite and well-researched article in the *Times of India* in which she has reviewed this book in great detail. Both Qamar Rais and late Sardar Jafri discussed the book in the conference of Progressive Writers' Association held at Hyderabad in 1996 and said very kind and encouraging words about it. We miss all of you and wish you were here to relish this moment with us.

We also express our thanks to Dr Khalid Ashraf and Arshad Gaur for their sustained interest and involvement in the publication of the Urdu edition of *Angarey* in 1995.

Most people in Delhi with any interest in literature, arts and aesthetics are bound to be acquainted with the awesome couple, Madhu and Rajan. To add to this is the fact that Madhu has been our colleague and friend in college for years. It was therefore most natural that they were amongst the first to read this translation. We are grateful for the zeal with which they responded. They made some extremely valuable suggestions that have contributed in enhancing the quality of this work.

We have also been extremely fortunate to have Rupa as

Acknowledgements

our publishers. We are especially indebted to Anurag Basnet whose keen understanding about the issues involved in the translation of a text like *Angarey* has been a revelation to us. He has worked along with us consistently and seriously, and without losing an iota of his pleasantness. Kadambari Mishra read through the manuscript with complete attention to all details. We are grateful to her for her suggestions. The translation would surely have been much poorer without them.

We spent long hours working in the college library. We are obliged to the staff of the library who have been forthcoming with continuous support in tracing out the books and the reference material we needed.

We would like to express our deep gratitude to our college, colleagues and students whose involvement in our work and faith in us has spurred and stimulated us to continue to work.

And finally, we do want to slip in a big thank you to our friends and families who have been an important part of our journey through this translation. Vir, Sukriti, Jaba, Hamd Irfan and Tabish Irfan—known together as 'Hamditabi'—thank you for being there and for taking care of all that we neglected while working on this translation.

Vibha S. Chauhan
Khalid Alvi

Milton Keynes UK
Ingram Content Group UK Ltd.
UKHW021414250824
1375UKWH00033B/289